MW01178113

Sanctuary

A Kate Redman Mystery: Book 8

Celina Grace

This book is for my mother-in-law,
Loletha Stoute, with my love.

Prologue

THE SUN GLITTERED ON THE sea, its beams penetrating the translucent blue waters as they broke upon the shore to touch the firm-packed sand below. Waves frilled with white foam hissed and sighed on the beach. They reached up to touch the larger pebbles, the driftwood and the drying seaweed before withdrawing back into the ocean, leaving the uncovered sand wet and gleaming for a second before the water sank away.

The body lay face downwards, arms lax and loose. An observer from the clifftop path, up above the beach, might have supposed the man to be an early morning sunbather, except sunbathers did not usually lie with their faces buried in the wet sand, and they were not usually clothed in ragged jeans and faded black T-shirts. If this hypothetical observer had descended the path onto the beach, and clashed and rattled over the pebbles before gaining the firmer ground of the sand, they would have seen the greyness of the exposed skin of the arms and the curious crab perched on one loosely-curled hand.

But there was no observer there that morning. There was no one on the beach at all, save for a crowd of seagulls wheeling overhead. The waves receded further as the tide went out, leaving the sad remains of what had once been a person lying alone, flung upon the sand like a piece of detritus discarded by the merciless sea.

Chapter One

THERE WERE WORSE WAYS TO wake up, Kate Redman thought dreamily, as she swam up out of sleep to find Tin's warm hand upon her, gently stroking. She rubbed the sleep from her eyes, turned over in bed, and kissed him. They were way past worrying about such things as morning breath now.

"You don't have to go in until later, do you?" murmured Tin, his lips to her shoulder and his hand moving lower.

"No," gasped Kate. "Not until ten."

"Fantastic..."

"Mmm..."

The ringing of Kate's mobile at that moment was particularly unwelcome. She did her best to ignore it, and keep her mind on what Tin was actually doing, until the strident ringing became so loud and insistent that she cursed and reached over to answer it.

"Oh, leave it," said Tin's muffled voice.

"You know I can't," said Kate. She gave him an apologetic look as he swam up from under the covers.

"Yeah, I know," he answered in a resigned tone. Kate pressed the answer icon on her phone screen. The name of the caller showed 'Anderton', something that gave her an unwelcome jolt, especially after what she'd just been doing.

"Sir?" she asked, trying to sound as composed as possible.

"Kate, hi. Sorry it's so early. Hope I didn't wake you up."

"You didn't, don't worry about it." Kate wondered what Anderton would say if she went on to tell him exactly what his phone call had interrupted. "What's up?"

As she said this, Tin's own phone started buzzing and skittering across the bedside table. He cursed and went to answer it. Kate swung her legs out of bed and headed for the relative privacy of the bathroom.

Anderton told her about the body that had been found. "Bit of a tricky one, this one."

"Why is that?"

"It's right on the edge of our jurisdiction. Might actually mean that we hand over to Salterton." Salterton was the neighbouring police force, based in the large coastal town that bore the name. "I don't know though yet, to be honest, and I'm taking us forward based on the premise that it's our case. Can you get here soon?"

"Of course." Kate balanced the phone between her chin and her shoulder as she twisted the shower controls to start the water flowing. "Just give me ten minutes to get ready. Where exactly are you?"

"I'll text you the postcode. SOCO are already here, and Mark's on his way."

"Fine," said Kate, testing the water temperature with her hand. "I'll be as quick as I can."

They said goodbye and Kate hopped into the shower. Over the noise of the rushing water, she could hear Tin's voice as he took his phone call but not what he was saying. As she rinsed the last of the lather from her legs, she saw the half open bathroom door open fully.

Tin handed her a towel. "I've got to go, Kate, sorry."

"That's okay, I've got to go myself." She didn't elaborate further; Tin knew she couldn't say much. Not that she knew much about what she was going to be investigating herself. A young black male, that was all Anderton had told her. A possible drowning, but possible foul play. Kate rubbed herself down briskly, thinking ahead.

Tin kissed her goodbye. "I'll see you later, yes? Maybe dinner somewhere?"

"That would be great, but who knows what time I'm going to get back? I'll call you, okay?"

"Okay." He gave her a final kiss. "And don't think I've forgotten where we were when we were so rudely interrupted."

Kate grinned. "I hope not."

Tin winked and waved as he headed out the door.

Smiling, Kate turned her attention to the bathroom mirror, trying to make herself look presentable, if not professional. As she powdered her face, she turned away a little from the mirror, so she could see herself in profile. The line of her left cheekbone showed a tiny dip that would now always be there. Kate ran a fingertip over it, sighing. At least it didn't hurt anymore. She thought of all the other injuries she'd sustained in the course of her career and thought, rather glumly, *you'll soon be able to* literally *read me like a map.* Then she squared her shoulders and dismissed the thought, preparing to face the day.

*

IT WAS A BEAUTIFUL AUTUMN day in early October. The sun shone brightly but the real warmth had gone and a whisper of the colder weather to come could be felt in the brisk breeze. Here and there, the trees were still green, but the leaves were faded and dull. The full autumnal range of colours was coming into play; a kaleidoscope of orange, gold, scarlet and ochre. Kate, remembering how windy it usually was at the seaside, stopped to pick up a scarf and a warmer jacket than she normally wore before flinging them on the back seat of her car.

It was about a forty minute drive to the coast from Abbeyford, the town in which she lived and worked. Muddiford Beach was a popular tourist attraction, although the large crowds of holidaymakers had dispersed a little now that the summer holidays were over. As Kate drew into the clifftop car park, she could see the blue and white police tape stretched over the entrance to the footpath that led from the top of the cliffs down to the beach. A couple of uniformed officers stood guard. She wrapped the scarf around her neck and locked the car, carrying her jacket in her hand.

Two hundred and forty steps led down to the beach, carved directly into the cliff. Kate negotiated each one with care, holding onto the railing on the beach side. Had the victim walked down these steps? Or had he come by boat? Had he even been thrown from the cliff top? Kate knew, as she walked over to where a white tent had been erected over the body, that if that were the case it would be obvious from the damage to the corpse. She ducked under the flap of the tent, bracing herself for the first sight.

The first person she saw was Chief Inspector Anderton. Detective Inspector Olbeck stood next to him, and the most recent recruit to the team, Detective Constable Anne Whittacker, was hanging back a little. Kate smiled at her as she walked forward. She liked her new colleague, a forty-something mother of three who'd returned to the career she'd left behind ten years ago to have children. Kate rather admired that—it couldn't have been easy, fitting back into full-time CID work, after a decade out of it.

"Morning," Anderton greeted her as Kate reached

them. For a moment, they all stood looking down at the body. It wasn't as bad as Kate had feared. If you looked at it with half-closed eyes, you could almost imagine the man was asleep. The illusion only lasted for a few seconds, though, once you took in the colour of the skin, the half-open eyes, the slackness of the mouth. He had been young, this man, no more than twenty-five, Kate thought. She crouched down to get a better view.

The body was dressed in tattered denim jeans and a faded black T-shirt. No socks, no shoes, no jewellery that Kate could see. She moved her gaze slowly from the paler soles of the feet, up over the torso, to the finely curved shape of the skull, clearly visible under the short black hair.

"Drowning?" she murmured, almost to herself.

Anderton crouched down next to her with a groan. "God, my knees. Getting too old for this." He gestured to the side of the head which was turned away from them into the sand. "It might be my eyes deceiving me but that doesn't look quite right to me. I think he's got head injuries." Kate looked at where he pointed and saw what he meant—what might have been a slight depression in the curve of the bone, a faint patch on the sand that could have been blood. "We'll know more once they've done the PM."

They both got up to their feet, Anderton slightly more stiffly than Kate.

"Any ID on the body?" Kate asked.

Olbeck shook his head. "We haven't found anything. And you know what else makes me pause?" They all looked at him. "Why isn't he wearing shoes?"

"It's a beach," Anne volunteered doubtfully. "Perhaps he took them off, up there." She pointed to the cliffs edging the beach.

"Maybe," said Olbeck, not sounding convinced. He stared hard at the worn clothes. "Maybe he was homeless."

"Maybe, maybe, maybe," said Anderton. There was a slight commotion at the entrance to the tent as what seemed like a crowd of people entered all at once. "Here's the rest of the cavalry."

Kate, Olbeck and Anne drew together a little, marking themselves out as a team, as five members of Salterton CID approached them. Kate didn't recognise any of them, except the DCI, George Atwell, who she remembered from his visit to Abbeyford as a rather podgy, jovial man. He didn't look very jovial now.

The five of the Salterton CID faced the four officers from Abbeyford. Kate could see various members of the SOCO team look up at the change in atmosphere.

"Anderton," said Atwell, making it sound like less a greeting and more a threat.

"Morning, George," replied Anderton, in a casual way that didn't fool Kate. She'd been in this situation once before, in her previous posting at Bournemouth. Two jurisdictions ostensibly collaborating on a case. What had *actually* happened was a whole lot of stepping on toes, offence taken and outright hostility. She hoped that wouldn't be the case here, but she had to admit it hadn't started off very promisingly.

As Atwell and Anderton thrashed out the preliminaries, Kate observed the Salterton team. There were three men, of various ages, and a woman of around Kate's own age, though she was very different in looks, being tall and blonde with an expression that Kate could only really describe as supercilious.

"Well, now, until we check the official boundaries, we don't know who needs to take this on," Anderton was saying in a conciliatory tone. Kate wondered why he was so eager to take this case anyway. She gave herself a quick mental kick for thinking it but it was inescapable. There was no way that this case would be high profile. The murder (if it was murder) of a poor, young, black man wouldn't rate anywhere near as highly as the killing of a young, white woman, for example. Kate caught herself thinking this and winced. That's why, Kate, she told herself crossly. That's why we need to take it on. If we don't care about the poor and the vulnerable, then who the hell will?

Brought back to reality, she realised that Atwell and Anderton were turning back to their own teams. She focused on what her DCI was saying.

"As I said before, team, we don't yet know who's going to have ultimate responsibility for this case. While we work that out, it's going to be more effective to work together." Kate risked a glance at the

Salterton team and wondered, from their frowning faces, whether they agreed with him. "DCI Atwell has kindly agreed to us debriefing with his own team, at the Salterton station, when we leave here."

There was no enthusiastic agreement to this—in fact, nobody said anything at all. Anderton continued. "We'll need someone from both teams to stay to see if there's anything from the preliminary medical exam."

"I will," said Kate, just as the blonde woman from the other team said the same thing. They looked at one another. Kate caught what she thought was the merest flicker of a sneer from the other woman, who lifted her chin and looked down her nose. What was *her* problem?

"You'd better introduce yourselves then," said Atwell, a smile finally breaking out on his round face.

"DS Kate Redman," said Kate, stepping forward and holding out her hand.

The blonde woman shook it limply, a mere squeeze of the fingers. "DS Chloe Wapping."

"Pleased to meet you," Kate said insincerely. Chloe said nothing but her mouth flickered in something that could have been a weak attempt at a smile. The two women stepped back to their respective teams.

Olbeck, ever the peacemaker, was already introducing himself to the other officers. At his easy manner, something of the strain went out of the situation and the atmosphere thawed slightly. Kate realised she had almost forgotten that they were all standing not ten feet from a dead body. She gave herself a quick mental shake, trying to focus her attention on what was important.

The pathologist, Doctor Gatkiss, had already arrived and was kneeling on the sand by the body. Kate suddenly had a thought and hurried over to Anderton.

"When does the tide turn? I mean, are we far enough up the beach for the sea not to reach the body?"

Anderton looked worried. "That's a good point, Kate." He looked up at the Salterton officers. "Anyone know? Do we have a tide chart or something?"

Having handed over that worry to her boss, Kate moved back to see what Doctor Gatkiss was doing. As she stood, silently watching, Chloe Wapping moved over to stand near her, just slightly too close for comfort. Try as she might, telling herself not to be paranoid, Kate couldn't help but feel that Chloe had done it on purpose. She shuffled back a few steps, trying to do it discreetly, only for Chloe to step forward again, closing the gap once more. She had a very faint smile on her face. Kate felt a muscle in her jaw twitch and turned her face away, pretending the other woman wasn't there.

"Good morning, Doctor Gatkiss," she said, thinking it wouldn't hurt to let Chloe know that she was quite friendly with the pathologist.

Ivor Gatkiss looked up and gave her his quick, shy smile. "Hello, DS Redman."

"How are you?"

"Very well, thank you. And you?"

Kate acknowledged that she was well. After a quick enquiry about another of the pathologists, Doctor Telling, now on maternity leave, Kate fell silent again, letting the doctor go on with his work.

The tent emptied out as the other officers left. Kate moved away from Chloe again and this time, walked away to observe the body from the other side. From this angle, she could see his face, half-buried in sand. Even in death, it was a striking face; high cheekbones, a strong jawline, a high-bridged nose. Who was he? Kate looked again at the ragged clothes in which he was dressed. They were dry, she realised. Did that mean anything, though? The body had lain in the sun for several hours; the tide was out.

"Do you think it's a suspicious death, Doctor?" she asked suddenly, ignoring the tiny hiss of breath from Chloe that could have been meant to indicate disbelief at Kate's directness.

Doctor Gatkiss looked up. He reminded Kate of a teddy bear, being rather burly and with a soft brown beard. "I believe so, yes. There's a strong indication that he died from head injuries. However, as you know, I really need to be able to perform a full post mortem before I can say with any certainty."

"Could he have drowned?" Chloe asked abruptly.

Both Kate and Doctor Gatkiss looked at her. "That is another possibility," said Doctor Gatkiss. "Again, the PM should tell us more." He sat back on his haunches for a moment, regarding the body. "However, the fact that the body is here, way above the tideline, suggests that if he *were* drowned, somebody has moved him further up the beach."

"And that's suspicious in itself," said Kate. Doctor Gatkiss nodded. Chloe said nothing.

After another twenty minutes, the doctor concluded his preliminary examination. One of his assistants had arrived and, between the two of them, the body was placed inside a body bag in preparation for transportation to the mortuary. Kate was crossing her fingers for a wallet being found in the pockets of the ragged jeans, perhaps a mobile phone or even a letter, something to give them some clue to the man's identity, but her hopes were dashed. He had nothing on him except the T-shirt and jeans he had died in.

Kate and Chloe watched the body being removed from the tent. Kate could hear the click and whirr of camera flashes outside and cursed inwardly. *Bloody press, here already...* She smoothed her windswept hair back as best she could and made her way to the tent entrance. Just as she was about to step out into the glare of the cameras, she was shouldered aside as Chloe pushed past her, out into daylight.

"No comment," was all the woman said as she walked past the small group of journalists and camera operators clustered outside the tent. Kate, flabbergasted, took a moment to pull herself together before walking outside herself. Now that Chloe had pre-empted her, Kate's mutter of 'no comment' sounded particularly weak. Kate, seething, was just preparing to walk through the crowd when she saw something that made her choke.

It was Tin, standing next to a tall, thin man who had a news camera up on his narrow shoulder. As Kate stood, gaping, the camera was swung towards her face.

"Detective, can you give us any more information about the crime scene?" Tin called, just as if he'd never met her before. "Is it true that the body might be that of an illegal immigrant?"

Stunned into silence, Kate took a moment to recover. Conscious that the shock on her face had been captured by the camera, she managed to pull herself together.

"There will be no official comment at this time," was all she said, but she hoped that the glare that accompanied expressed a lot of what she wanted to say.

"Might this be a victim of the people-smuggling gangs that have been operating in the area recently?" Tin persisted.

"I said, *no comment*," Kate snapped. She turned sharply and began to stalk towards the distant cliff path, clenching her fists. She could see Chloe's blonde head ahead of her, already halfway up the steps.

In the sanctuary of her car, Kate rested her head on the steering wheel and took a number of deep breaths. What the hell was Tin playing at? It was a situation that had never occurred before. Why the hell was he reporting on this story, and for whom? Did he actually expect Kate to give him an exclusive? Kate raised shaking hands to her head again, smoothing her hair compulsively. And as for Chloe, what the hell was her problem? Kate found herself thinking back over the past hour. Had she inadvertently done something to offend the other woman? Or was she, Chloe, just a moody bitch? *Deep breaths, Kate.*

It was a few moments before she recollected that she was supposed to be heading for the Salterton station and not back to Abbeyford. Starting the engine, she drove slowly out of the clifftop carpark, frowning.

Chapter Two

Kate had been driving for several minutes, negotiating the unfamiliar roads, when something that Tin had said reoccurred to her. *Might this be a victim of the people-smuggling gangs that have been operating in the area recently?*

There was a lay-by at the side of the road, a viewing spot to enable cars to park to take in the spectacular views over the coastline. Kate flicked on the indicator and pulled the car over. She sat with her chin on the steering wheel, staring unseeing out of the windscreen, oblivious to the magnificent vista of sky and sand and sea before her. She was deep in thought. Of course, *now* she remembered. Tin had been working on a feature for one of the national papers: about the refugee crisis worsening every day in mainland Europe and the growing problem of people-smuggling that was beginning to affect this area of the coast. He'd only just returned from a research trip to Calais, gathering stories from the people living in the refugee camps there. Kate thought back to the body on the beach, remembering the ragged clothes, the lack of identification. Could the man have drowned crossing the Channel in an unsafe boat, a dinghy that overturned in the choppy waters as it crossed into the bay? Kate remembered Doctor Gatkiss talking about the possible head injuries that victim had suffered. Could they have been inflicted after death, the body tumbling against sharp rocks as it washed into the bay and onto the beach? But then, if that were the case, how did it end up above the tideline?

If the body was that of an illegal migrant, or a refugee, then that made the chance of identification that much harder. Kate pushed herself upright again, shook herself mentally, and began to turn the car around to re-join the road. The debrief would probably be over by the time she got to Salterton station. As if on cue, a text message sounded on her phone and when she opened it, she could see if was from Olbeck. *All over here, head back to Abbeyford when you're ready.* With a mingled feeling of relief and annoyance, Kate began the drive back to her home town.

*

EVERYONE WAS BACK AT THEIR desks by the time Kate reached the office. She made a bee-line for Olbeck's office, shutting the door behind her. "How did it go at Salterton?"

Olbeck looked up from his keyboard. "Fine, I think," he said, somewhat absently. Kate made a noise of disbelief which made him look at her a little more closely. "Okay, so there was a little bit of awkwardness—"

"Ha!"

"Come on, they're not that bad."

"That Chloe Wapping is. Believe me. Do you know, I think she was actually crowding me on purpose?"

"What do you mean?"

"I mean, every time I moved away from her, she came even closer. Just to piss me off."

Olbeck gave her a wry look. "Are you sure?"

Kate sighed and flumped down in the chair opposite his. "Well, perhaps. I don't know what her problem is, so I'm ignoring it, for now. Do we have a definite answer yet on whose case it is?"

"Nope. Still deciding."

"Wonderful." Kate pushed her hair off her face with both hands. "You'll never guess who collared me as soon as I stepped out of the tent, as well?"

"Amanda Hargreaves?" This was a local journalist known for her stinging criticism of the local police force in cases she perceived they were taking a little too long to solve.

"Worse. Tin."

Olbeck's eyebrows shot up. "Oh. That must have been awkward."

"That's one way of putting it."

Olbeck frowned. "He's doing that feature though, isn't he? On the refugees coming into Bristol?"

Kate nodded. "If he thinks he's going to get anything from me on this case, he's got another think coming."

Olbeck looked uncomfortable. "Oh, I'm sure he knows full well you won't be able to tell him anything."

"Hmmm." Kate was fidgeting with a pen that had been lying on the edge of Olbeck's desk. She clicked the point in and out as she spoke. "Anyway, it did make me think about our John Doe..."

"What, that you think he might be a refugee too?"

Kate caught his eye. "Well, it certainly seems possible, doesn't it? It's not the first time we've had a body washed up on a beach..." She trailed off. She wondered if Olbeck was thinking what she was thinking, remembering the gut wrenching pictures of the young Syrian children who had drowned attempting to reach the Greek island of Kos, the pictures that had begun to galvanise the entire recent refugee support movement.

That had been the only time Kate had ever seen Olbeck cry at work. She'd come into his office, one morning, and found him staring down at the newspaper, with those awful pictures on the front cover, head in his hands and tears running down his face.

She tried to purge her mind of the images and thought back to what she'd seen this morning. "I suppose we won't know much more until the PM," she said slowly. "Do you want me to attend that?"

"If you could. No doubt DS Wapping will make her way there."

"What fun," Kate said ironically.

"I suppose there's a very faint chance we might be able to do a DNA match, or a dental match for ID."

Kate nodded. "Perhaps we shouldn't be jumping to conclusions right away. He could very well be British."

"Exactly. I'll debrief Anderton, and let me know what comes up at the PM."

Kate threw him a grin and a salute and made her way back to her desk. She heard the buzz of another text message come through to her phone as she sat down and fished it out of her bag. There was a text message from Tin. Setting her jaw, Kate opened it to read it. *Sorry*, the message ran. *Shouldn't have sprung that on you but didn't realise your team was there! Let's talk later xxx.*

Not deigning to reply, Kate threw her phone back into her handbag and turned to her computer. After a few minutes of staring blankly at her computer screen, she took her phone back out of her bag and looked again at Tin's message. Seriously? He was sorry? Did he actually imagine for one minute that Kate would be able to tell him absolutely anything about this case? She found herself gritting her teeth again and consciously made herself relax and breathe out.

She knew that the refugee cause was one close to Tin's heart. Himself the son of a Nigerian immigrant, who'd arrived in the late sixties to work in the National

Health Service, Tin also had several friends who had claimed asylum after fleeing war and persecution abroad. He'd been following the story of the refugee crisis for some months before it became something of national importance, and Kate knew that he'd been investigating claims of people-smuggling along the coast from Bristol and its surrounding ports. It was also something that she knew Anderton was aware of, although responsibility for monitoring the situation came under the jurisdiction of Border Control and its allied departments.

It wasn't that Kate was unsympathetic to both Tin's view and to the problems faced by the migrants and refugees. It was just that this was the first time in their relationship that her personal life had suddenly and violently impacted upon her professional life. It was bound to happen sooner or later, she told herself rather bleakly, staring at her computer screen. *You'll just have to learn to deal with it.* Once more, she took her phone out of her bag and stared again at the screen. Laboriously, she typed out a long reply, trying to convey her shock at seeing Tin there at the scene, at being questioned by him live on air, trying to get across just how difficult it was going to make things between them...before deleting it all and typing a simple sentence. *Will be late home so will talk tomorrow.*

"Ah, Kate," said a voice behind her, making her jump. She hurriedly put her phone away and turned around to see Detective Chief Inspector Anderton standing behind her, one foot tapping impatiently on the floor.

"Sir?"

"What's the low down on our body on the beach?"

Kate glanced across at Olbeck, still hunched over his desk. He clearly hadn't had a chance to talk to their immediate boss yet. "Not much to go on, as yet. It's a young man, probably of African or West Indian ethnicity, maybe twenty-five or so."

"Cause of death?"

"Possible head injuries, but he might also have drowned. Doctor Gatkiss is doing the PM tomorrow."

"You'll head along to that, won't you?"

Kate nodded. Then she asked, cautiously, "Do we know if it's our case or not yet?"

Anderton rolled his eyes. "Unfortunately, Kate, I have a feeling this might be a joint effort. I'm liaising with Atwell on this very matter at the moment."

Kate repressed a groan with an effort, thinking about undertaking an investigation with DS Chloe 'I'm a sour-faced cow' Wapping on her back throughout it all. Anderton grinned suddenly. "I'm sure it'll be fine, whatever happens."

"Right," said Kate, trying to keep the sarcasm from her tone. Anderton tipped her a wink and went on his way, over to Olbeck's office.

Kate heard her phone buzz again and somehow

knew it was Tin before even reading what he'd said. She grabbed her phone from her bag. Yes, she was right.

Thought we were having dinner tonight? he'd written.

It was Kate's turn to roll her eyes. She texted back *Not tonight. Am flat out with this new case, as you should well know. Talk tomorrow.* After a moment, she added a grudging kiss on the end of the message. Then she sent it, turned her phone off and, squaring her shoulders, finally got down to work.

Chapter Three

THERE WAS A SURPRISE IN store for Kate when she arrived at the pathology labs the next morning. She opened the door to the examination room, noting with satisfaction that Chloe Wapping hadn't yet arrived, and then saw who was bending over the shrouded body on the table.

"Andrew!" she said in shock. "What a surprise! I didn't realise you were back in the country."

Doctor Andrew Stanton had once been a boyfriend of Kate's, a long time ago. He smiled and greeted her pleasantly. "We flew back last month."

'We' clearly meant Andrew and his wife, who Kate hadn't met. She smiled in a neutral fashion, and moved to stand over by the side of the room, but Andrew was clearly in a chatty mood.

"I'm not sure if you've heard but we're expecting our first in March next year."

"Your first?" repeated Kate and then the penny dropped. "Oh, Andrew, congratulations, that's fantastic news." She was pleased to find that she was genuinely happy for him.

"Thanks, we're very happy at the news. That's mostly why I decided to come back here, give Junior somewhere a bit more stable to grow up." Andrew had worked in Sierra Leone for several years. "Still, exciting news, eh?" He snapped on his gloves. "You're looking well, by the way."

"Oh, thanks," said Kate, a little flustered. She watched as Andrew threw back the green sheet that covered the body. As always, the sight of the corpse drove every other thought out of Kate's head for a moment. The body looked smaller than she remembered, diminished in death.

"Now, what have we here?" asked Andrew, rhetorically. He bent to his work just as the door to the room opened and Chloe Wapping walked in. Kate was pleased to see that she looked rather flushed and hurried.

"DS Chloe Wapping," said Chloe, panting a little.

Andrew looked at Kate in some confusion which only increased when Chloe added "Salterton CID."

"It's a joint investigation," Kate said, thinking she may as well start getting used to the idea. As yet, Chloe hadn't even acknowledged she was in the room.

"Oh right," said Andrew. "Well, let's get started, shall we?"

Kate and Chloe watched in silence. Kate thought about how odd it was to observe Andrew now and thought about when they were a couple, and how long ago it now seemed, almost as if it had happened to someone else. She also thought, rather gloomily, that she *did* seem to be able to have successful relationships with men—as long as she wasn't romantically or sexually involved with them in any way.

That thought brought Tin to her mind, but she was still too cross with him for the memory to bring her any pleasure. She shifted position a little. Chloe was still successfully acting as if she and Andrew were alone in the room.

"Any indications of drowning?" Chloe asked, rather abruptly. Andrew looked rather annoyed at the interruption.

"None whatsoever," he said, shortly.

"So what is the cause of death?"

For a moment Andrew looked as though he wasn't going to answer. Then he said, stiffly, "The victim died of head trauma. There were several blows to the occipital area of the skull causing a skull depression, inter-cranial bleeding and other damage to the brain."

"So what was he hit with? Or could it have been accidental?"

Kate caught Andrew's eye from behind Chloe's back and rolled her own gaze up to the ceiling. That brought a flicker of a smile onto his face and he answered Chloe in a tone that was slightly less cold. "I very much doubt it was accidental. The shape of the wounds, and the damage to the scalp, suggests that whatever he was hit with was smooth-sided, not jagged like a rock. As there are no indications of drowning, it seems very unlikely that the head injuries would have been suffered whilst in the water."

Kate was trying to recall the crime scene, picturing the body as it lay sprawled on the seashore. "There weren't any big rocks near his head, not that I can remember," she said, almost to herself. "And he was too far from the cliff face for it to have been a rock fall."

Chloe had no response to this other than a sniff. Andrew, who was labelling various sample pots, looked up. "Whatever the weapon was, it was smooth, probably round—something like a baseball bat, or a round stick or something like that."

Kate pondered. "Are there any fragments of anything in the wound? Splinters, anything like that?"

"Not that I can see. A quantity of sand, minute fragments of seaweed, but certainly nothing embedded in the actual wound."

They all lapsed back into silence as Andrew continued the examination. Kate was thinking. If the weapon had been something like a rock, then that would have suggested that the murder had been impulsive, unplanned. But—if she was correct in remembering the crime scene as it was—there was nothing in the vicinity of the body that fitted the description of the weapon Andrew had given. Of course, the search of the beach was still underway, so perhaps something would be found. But if the perpetrator had brought along a baseball bat, or a poker, or something like that, surely that suggested that this murder had been planned and premeditated?

At long last, Andrew finished his work, pulled off his gloves and threw them into the hazardous waste bin with the air of a man glad to have completed an unpleasant task. Not for the first time, Kate wondered what it was like to be a pathologist, to spend every working day up to your elbows in dead bodies. What must it be like to go home to your family, having spent the day cutting into a corpse? One thing was for sure, thought Kate, Andrew probably didn't enjoy too many Sunday roasts. She bit back a grin and stood up, slinging her bag over her shoulder.

She hadn't expected Chloe to say goodbye and in this expectation, she was not disappointed. The other woman had muttered something to Andrew which might have been 'thanks' and then left without another word. Andrew finished drying his hands and turned to Kate with his eyebrows raised. "What the hell is her problem?"

"I'm glad it's not just me who thinks that," Kate said, half-smiling. "And the answer is: I have no idea."

"I mean, God knows I know some officers can be a bit prickly—"

"That's true—"

"Especially the female ones," Andrew finished, with a grin.

Kate laughed. "Yes, well, they can't be all as lovely as me."

It was Andrew's turn to laugh. "Well, I'd better get

on. It was nice to see you again, Kate. Why not come round to dinner sometime?"

"I'd like that," Kate said, genuinely meaning it. She said goodbye and left with a cheery wave. Despite having just suffered both Chloe's presence and a post-mortem, Kate felt quite light-hearted, for a change. If Andrew still wanted to be friends with her, then surely she couldn't have behaved that badly towards him? Humming a little tune, she walked down the corridor towards the carpark with a light step.

The first thing she saw when she came out of the building was Chloe Wapping standing by what was obviously her car, looking red-faced and furious. Kate, startled by the expression on her face, momentarily thought of marching by without making eye contact but as they were parked side by side, that would have been quite awkward.

She steeled herself as she walked up to her own car and asked, "What's wrong?"

"My bloody car's broken down." Chloe looked as though she was restraining herself from aiming a kick at the tires. "That's why I was late this morning. Now it's conked out completely."

"Oh dear," said Kate, trying without much success to force some sincerity into her voice. She was silent for a moment, thinking fast. Going very much against the grain of what she wanted to do, she said, "Do you want a lift somewhere?"

Chloe's face showed a momentary struggle. "No, I'm fine," she said, after a second's pause.

"Okay," Kate said lightly. She pointed her keys at her own car, unlocking it. "I suppose you're waiting for the breakdown people, is that it?"

Chloe grunted something. Kate got into her car and prepared to drive off, trying not to let the schadenfreude she was currently experiencing show on her face.

She had put the car in gear and was preparing to reverse when a sudden knock on her closed window made her jump and almost stall the car. She took her foot off the clutch and opened the window.

Chloe was bending forward, looking both cross and worried. "Look, I—would you—I have to be somewhere, and I can't be late. Is there—would you be able—"

Kate sighed inwardly. "Hop in." She leant over to the passenger door to open it.

Driving away from the pathology labs, the atmosphere and the silence in the car thickened. Kate was already regretting her impulsive offer. She didn't even know where she was supposed to be going.

"Where do you need to go?"

She felt, rather than saw, Chloe glance at her. There was a long moment of silence before Chloe said rather reluctantly, "Muddiford Beach."

Kate glanced back at her in surprise. "You're going back to the scene?"

"No. You need to drive on a bit further than the beach carpark. I'll direct you once we get closer."

Kate shifted a little in her seat, easing her shoulders. "What are you going to be doing there?"

For a moment, she thought Chloe was going to tell her to mind her own business. Then she spoke, obviously with extreme reluctance. "There's a witness who lives about half a mile away from the beach who thinks he may have seen something on the night of the murder."

Shock made Kate wobble a little on the road. Correcting the car's direction, she tried to keep the anger out of her voice when she said, "Were you planning on sharing this information with us?"

Chloe said nothing. Kate, with no better method of expressing her annoyance at the moment, breathed in sharply through her nose.

She said nothing else for the next ten minutes. After that, her curiousity got the better of her. "Who's the witness?"

"He's a retired harbourmaster. Now he volunteers for the Muddiford Beach Trust, so he knows the area well."

"How did you track him down?" Kate didn't add what she was thinking, which was *how come we didn't track him down too?*

"He called us," Chloe said in a bored voice. She turned her face away to look out of the window, and

Kate got the impression that that was all she was going to be saying for a while. They drove the rest of the way in a mutually resentful silence.

Chapter Four

THE RETIRED HARBOURMASTER'S NAME WAS Alan Hardcastle. He was a small, wiry man with untidy white hair and faded blue eyes, his skin roughened by years of sea winds and harsh weather. His cottage on the cliff-top, the only one for miles around, was charming: built of white-painted local stone and surrounded by a garden in which coastal plants abounded.

"It was midnight," he said, once they were seated in the living room and he'd offered refreshments that both Kate and Chloe had refused. "I normally go to bed earlier than that, but I'd been watching a good film on TV so that was why I was up later than normal. I'd just turned the kitchen light out and was pulling the blind down when I saw someone walking down the steps to the beach. I've got a good view of the beach—here, let me show you..."

They all moved to the kitchen, and both Kate and Chloe peered out of the large kitchen window. Muddiford Beach and the cliff-top steps were unmistakeable. Kate could see that the evidence tent was still there, the white markers placed by the Scene of Crime officers just about visible from this distance.

"It would have been dark, Mr Hardcastle," she said, turning to face him. "What exactly could you see?"

"You're right, I couldn't see much, but I definitely saw a figure holding a torch, walking down the steps. Obviously, I couldn't see him clearly but he looked tall, quite young in the way he moved."

Kate was sceptical that he could have even deduced that much. The bobbing light of a handheld torch, yes, but to see anything other than that, in the pitch dark and at this distance? She realised Mr Hardcastle was still speaking.

"That first fella, he came down the steps and onto the beach and waited, it looked like. Of course, by then I was interested because you know we get smugglers sometimes along this coast, drugs and people smugglers. Well, you lot would know about that, I suppose. Anyway, I was staring out and then another person came down the steps, also with a torch. It looked like he met up with the other fella and they walked off round the curve of the cliff and then I lost sight of them."

"Could you describe the second figure, Mr Hardcastle?" Chloe asked.

"Not really, I'm afraid. Just like the other one, all you could really see was a tall, dark figure."

"You say you think you saw two men, are you

certain of that? Could one or both of them have been a woman?"

Mr Hardcastle pondered, his wrinkled mouth pulled in. Then he shrugged. "I couldn't really say, to be honest. I suppose I just assumed it was two men, I mean, why would a woman be down there in the dead of night?"

Why would a man be? Kate thought that and then laughed at herself. That was exactly what they were trying to find out, wasn't it?

"Thank you, Mr Hardcastle," said Chloe. She was speaking in a gentler and more polite tone of voice than Kate had yet heard from her. "Is there anything else you can remember?"

The old man thought for a few moments and then shook his head. "I don't think so. It's not much to go on, I know... They didn't come back, or at least, they didn't while I was still watching. I gave up after about twenty minutes and went to bed. I was tired."

Kate wanted to ask him why he hadn't called the police, if he'd been worried, but didn't want it to sound like an accusation. And really, there wasn't any law about walking on the beach at midnight if you felt the inclination, was there? There were a hundred explanations for the two figures; secret lovers, a drug deal, even perhaps some nocturnal wildlife watching... It was just the fact that this sighting had occurred on the night before the body had been discovered that made it potentially important.

Chloe was talking. "It would be great if you could come along to Salterton Station at some point this week, Mr Hardcastle, and make a statement to the effect of what you've just told me." She shot a look at Kate as if daring her to try and get him to come to Abbeyford instead. Kate stared back, impassive, and Chloe went on to thank Mr Hardcastle for being so public-spirited.

Again, once they were driving away in the car, silence fell. Kate was conscious of the great mass of water to her left as they drove along the cliff top road, past the car park and the path that led down to Muddiford Beach. It was a glorious day and the sun glittered off the surface of the sea in a million glistening points of light.

"So, I'll drop you back in Salterton, then?" she asked, repressing the sharp retort that wanted to tack itself on the end of the sentence; *unless you've got any other shady interviews set up that your co-workers aren't aware of.*

"Yes."

"That's *no* problem," said Kate, sarcasm getting the better of her for once.

Chloe said nothing but the thickened quality of the silence in the car worsened even more. Kate drove on, her mood darkening. How did Anderton expect his team to get anywhere with this case if their co-workers wouldn't even discuss the case? She tightened her grip on the steering wheel. Was it even worth bothering to ask the question she wanted to? She mentally gritted her teeth and then asked aloud ,"So, what do you think might have happened?"

Chloe said nothing for a moment. Then she said slowly and with some hostility in her voice, "I don't know. It's too early to say."

How helpful. Kate drove on, chastising herself for even bothering to make the effort to talk. She was surprised when Chloe asked her the same question a second later.

"What do I think?" was her response, so startled was she to hear a reasonably polite question from the woman sat next to her that she repeated what Chloe had just asked her.

"Yes."

"Well, I—" Kate floundered for a second. "You're right in that it's probably too early to say anything with definition. But—" she pressed on, seeing Chloe begin to sneer again at her indecisiveness. "I've been thinking about the weapon."

"Yes?" Chloe asked, guardedly.

"Andrew—Doctor Stanton—said it was something smooth-sided, rounded, like a bat or a stick, right?"

"Right." Chloe sounded a bit more interested.

"Well, what if those men that Hardcastle saw were actually involved? What were they carrying?"

"Carrying?" Chloe looked at her without comprehension for a minute and then Kate saw her face clear. "Torches!"

"Yep," said Kate, pleased. "What if the weapon was a torch, you know, one of those big heavy metal ones?"

Chloe sounded more enthusiastic than Kate had ever heard her. "That's a good idea, actually. That sounds eminently feasible."

Kate hid her grin, concentrating on the road. For a moment, she felt a flicker of lightness—this was the first time that she'd felt any kind of connection with Chloe, the first time their conversation had approached anything like partnership. After a moment, she added, casually, "Of course, that also brings up the question of whether the crime was premeditated or not. If the murder weapon was a torch, then it doesn't sound very likely that the murder was planned, does it? I mean, it's not exactly the first thing you'd think of as a weapon, is it?"

Chloe drummed her fingers on her black-clad knee, her face eager and devoid of its usual sneer. "We'd need to be able to prove it. We'd still have to find the weapon and match it to the wounds."

"I know." Kate didn't bother to point out that finding the weapon would be the hardest part. She also noted that Chloe had used 'we' for the first time.

For a moment, the energy in the car seemed to swell and then, as they drove on, somehow it flickered and died. Kate could feel Chloe withdrawing once more, turning back into the cold, distant figure that she'd always been. Kate's mood dipped simultaneously and they drove back to Salterton Station in silence.

Kate pulled up outside the main entrance and Chloe opened the passenger door. Kate didn't know whether she expected a 'goodbye' or not, or even a 'thanks' and for a second, as Chloe went to shut the car door without a word, felt a wave of anger at the woman's bad manners. Then Chloe opened the door again and stuck her head back into the car.

"Look," she said whilst Kate looked at her in surprise. "I don't like being paired with you any more than you like being paired with me, okay? But if we're going to get anywhere with this case, we just have to make the best of it, okay?"

Kate was so flabbergasted that for a second she was robbed of speech. She mouthed inarticulately for a second before the anger that she'd been repressing all day came flooding up into her mouth. "I never said anything about being upset about being paired with you, for Christ's sake. And if I do have a problem with it, it's because you're so bloody rude!"

Chloe pulled her head back, as if stung, and Kate snatched the car door handle and slammed the door shut. She pulled away from the kerb with an angry roar of the engine and didn't look back to see if Chloe was watching her do it.

Chapter Five

KATE PASSED A RESTLESS NIGHT and got up reluctantly the next morning. The weather, dramatically changed from yesterday, didn't help her mood. The sky was oppressively grey and from time to time, little spats of rain fell. The fallen autumn leaves lay in soggy heaps on the pavement, and Kate paused at the entrance to Abbeyford Station to detach a large yellow chestnut leaf that had plastered itself to her shoe.

On entering the office, she began to feel better. After Chloe's hideous manners, it was such a relief to see some friendly, familiar faces that it was with difficulty that she restrained herself from throwing her arms around Theo in gratitude after he greeted her with his customary, 'wotcha'.

"Coffee, mate?"

"Yes please, large and strong—" She mimicked what Theo was saying in a bored tone, "Yes, *like I like my men*." He gave her a wink and a grin and she burst out laughing despite herself. "God, it's good to be back here after a day with Salterton's finest, I can tell you that for nothing."

"Oh, is *that* what you got up to yesterday, eh? Fraternising with the enemy?" Theo handed her a steaming mug and she took it with gratitude. "Which one were you with?"

"Chloe Wapping."

"That hot blonde chick? How come I get the fat old git and you get the sexy one?"

Kate rolled her eyes. "Looks aren't everything, Theo. *Especially* in her case. Seriously."

"Yeah, well, I'd still like the opportunity to come to my own conclusion, you know..."

They bickered amiably back and forth for a few minutes as the office filled up around them. Olbeck blew Kate a kiss as he hurried past to his office, where he shut the glass door and dialled a number on his phone. Clearly on a conference call, then, Kate thought. She turned back to face the door, as she could hear Hurricane Anderton approaching in his own inimitable style.

"Morning, team. Morning, team." He offloaded the pile of cardboard folders he'd been carrying onto an adjacent desk. "Hope you're all raring to go this morning." His eyes fell on Kate, who sat up a little straighter. "Hello there, Kate, glad to see you've decided to grace us with your presence this morning."

It could have been a rebuke but he was smiling, so Kate thought she could be a little bit cheeky in her reply. "Well, I didn't really have anything better to do, so..."

Grinning, Anderton hoisted himself onto the desk. "Right, I do know that you went to the PM yesterday. Anything of interest to report? Definite cause of death?"

"Yes—and yes." Kate explained, as succinctly as she could, Andrew Stanton's findings, finishing up with what he'd told her about the type of murder weapon they should be looking for. "I don't suppose the beach search turned up anything that might be what we're looking for?"

Anderton shook his head regretfully. "Sadly not, but we weren't really expecting to find it, were we? Perp probably just flung it out to sea and it sank to the bottom of the ocean. I wonder? If it were a knife or something like that, it might be worth getting some divers down there...hmmm... Food for thought..." He scribbled something in the notebook he had next to him on the desk.

Kate waited until it was clear that he wasn't going to say anything else and then went on with her story. "The DS from Salterton, Chloe Wapping, and I went to interview a potential witness, an Alan Hardcastle—" She was interrupted by a splutter from Rav. "What's up, Rav?"

"He was on my list of interviewees this morning. How did they get hold of him so quickly?"

Kate pulled one shoulder up into a shrug. "DS

Wapping said he'd called them. Salterton, I mean. I suppose they are nearer, geographically..."

Rav looked annoyed. "It's probably not worth me going again, is it, guv?" He looked to Anderton for confirmation. "Unless you think it is?"

Anderton shrugged. "Liaise with Kate. She should be able to tell you whether it's worth your while." Rav looked over at Kate, who tried to give him an encouraging smile. She mouthed 'after this' and Rav nodded in understanding. He still looked rather cross.

There was a short silence while Anderton scribbled something else down. "Anything else?" he asked eventually, scanning the room.

Anne Whittacker raised her hand. Kate observed her, noting that as usual she was very carefully, if discreetly, made-up. Where did she find the time? Kate, who didn't wear much make-up, still found it a struggle to apply the bare minimum that she did every morning. She had been known to apply eye-shadow using her rear-view mirror once she'd parked the car in the morning. Anne had three children to get ready for school every work day and she still managed to do the full face-work, so she clearly had awe-inspiring time management skills. Perhaps I can ask her for a few tips, Kate thought.

"I've checked MISPER," Anne was saying, referring to the Missing Persons database. "There were a few possibilities on there, at first glance, but once I'd checked more thoroughly, they didn't stack up. None of the ages were right, for a start."

Anderton nodded. "So, our victim hasn't been reported missing. Yet. Disappointing, but not altogether unexpected. Thanks for checking, Anne." Anne smiled, obviously pleased at the compliment. Anderton went on. "Anyone know if there's CCTV in that beach carpark?"

"There isn't," said Theo.

"Damn. That would have been helpful, particularly after what Kate's told us about the possible suspect sighting. Never mind. Can someone—Theo, if you don't mind—double check where the nearest cameras are and see what footage you can pull from that night?"

"Sure," said Theo,

"What about a press conference?" Kate asked. "Could we make a public appeal for information?"

Anderton rubbed his chin, looking thoughtful. "That's a good idea, although I'm not sure it'll be granted for this type of murder. The chief gets a bit funny about setting them up for anything other than kiddies and abductions. Still—" he added, as Kate looked as though she was going to protest. "What we can definitely do is do a general media release, asking for information, giving the general details."

By this time, Olbeck had finished his conference call and had come to join the team. He slipped onto the bench, sitting next to Kate. "We don't have a photograph, though, do we? They're not going to use an image of a corpse."

Anderton grimaced. "No. True."

"Couldn't IT do some digital jiggery-pokery?" asked Kate. "You know, use the post-mortem photograph of the face but alter it a little so it doesn't look quite so... dead?"

Anderton did not look convinced. "I'm not sure. Ethically... Well, perhaps we can look into it, at least. Kate, would you mind?"

Kate nodded. "I'll have a word with Sam after this."

"Good." Anderton sprang to his feet and began to gather up his notebooks. "Right, PM report should be here today or tomorrow. I want you all to read through that. The same goes for any forensic reports that come through. We'll debrief again tomorrow and if anyone needs me, I'm here until about two o'clock this afternoon." He paused, halfway out of the door. "Anything else before I shoot off?"

Olbeck had got to his feet too. "I'm taking Kate with me to interview the manager of the Refugee Support Centre. You know, in Salterton."

Anderton paused, obviously surprised. Then he nodded. "Might be a bit premature but—no, no, give it a go." He grinned. "At least we might get there before our Salterton friends think of it. Right, well, carry on, get the evidence, you know the drill." He gave a vague wave with his free hand as he disappeared around the corner of the corridor.

Kate thought of Chloe Wapping and wondered briefly what the sour-faced cow was currently up to. Hunting down more witnesses? She had a brief memory of how Chloe's voice had changed when they'd interviewed the elderly Alan Hardcastle, how it had softened and become more gentle. So she clearly *was* capable of politeness—just clearly not to Kate. Kate made an effort to dismiss Chloe from her mind and concentrated on the agreeable prospect of an investigation with Olbeck.

"Ready?" he said a moment later, as if he'd read her mind.

"Just let me talk to Sam first, about that photograph."

She quickly ran down the stairs to the basement, where the IT department was located. Sam Hollington had been promoted several times since Kate had first met him, all those years ago, when they were investigating the murder of Elodie Duncan. Although he was now quite senior, he still retained a mop of dark curls and the cheerful round face that made him such a favourite with Kate.

"Morning, Sam," she said, popping her head around his booth. The screensaver image on his computer was a still from *Jurassic World*, a ferocious dinosaur splaying its jaws full of razor-sharp teeth. Someone had written on a Post-It note, 'Anderton before coffee', with an arrow pointing to the dinosaur's head. Kate grinned.

After a quick conversation, the outcome of which

was that Sam promised to do what he could to get them a media-acceptable image of the dead man, Kate thanked him and sprang back upstairs, eager to be out in the fresh air and on her way to the interview.

She was just grabbing up her coat when she remembered she was supposed to be speaking to Rav too. Quickly, she looked at his desk but he wasn't there or anywhere she could see in the office. Kate scribbled a note telling him to call her if he needed to and then hurried towards the door.

"Where are we going again?" she asked Olbeck, once they were on their way.

"The Salterton Refugee Support Centre. It was set up last year to help deal with all the migrants and asylum seekers who were turning up."

"Who set it up? The council?"

Olbeck kept glancing at the sat nav, checking which way they were supposed to be going. "No, it's a charity thing, what's the name of it? Sanctuary, that's it. They run another one in London and one in Kent, I think."

"Oh yes." Kate watched as they drove past Salterton Police Station and fought the childish urge to give it the finger. "So, you still think our victim is a refugee?"

Olbeck looked over at her. "Well—it's a definite possibility, isn't it? I hope I'm wrong. It'll be absolute hell, trying to get an identification, if the poor bugger's come over here from Syria or wherever without any papers."

"He didn't look like he was from Syria."

"Well, who knows? I've got the PM photos, so maybe someone will recognise him."

"Yes, I know." Kate realised she sounded rather negative. Perhaps Chloe Wapping had influenced her more than she had realised. "It's definitely worth a try."

They chatted about other things for the rest of the drive. Olbeck confided, rather hesitatingly, that he and Jeff, his husband, were thinking of trying to adopt a child. Kate knew he hesitated because of what she'd experienced, and how she'd reacted when he'd previously shared this news. She felt a jab of shame at the memory. She hastened to reassure him, by her tone and her enthusiastic questions, that she didn't mind one bit. She genuinely hoped that he and Jeff would be able to have a family.

"I'm as nervous as hell about it," Olbeck admitted. "It's supposed to be such a stressful, intrusive process. But it's something we really want to do."

"I'll help in any way I can," Kate said stoutly, and she meant every word. Her reward was Olbeck's grateful smile.

Chapter Six

THE SUPPORT CENTRE WAS A long, low building, probably built in the late seventies or early eighties. There were a number of huge, wheeled bins arranged along the side of one exterior wall. As Kate and Olbeck walked towards the entrance, Kate realised that the bins weren't full of rubbish, as she'd first supposed, but were full to the brim with bags of clothes, shoes, blankets and what looked like children's toys. Some were so full that a few bags had tumbled to the ground and were heaped up on the concrete.

"Oh, people have been incredibly generous," said the harassed looking, middle-aged woman who greeted them as they walked into the building. "Really, too generous, almost. What we really need is a few more warm bodies to help us sort all this *stuff*." She waved a hand towards what was obviously another store-room, again full to bursting with clothes, shoes, wellington boots, tins of food, blankets and other items. It was rather like being at a giant jumble sale.

"Are you here to volunteer?" She looked so hopeful Kate hated to disappoint her.

"I'm afraid we're here because we need to talk to the manager," Olbeck said, pulling it out his badge and warrant card. The woman's face reflected her shock. "It's fine," Olbeck reassured her. "No one's in any trouble. We're just after some information."

The woman rallied somewhat. "I'll just fetch Ruth," she murmured faintly and left the foyer almost at a run.

Kate and Olbeck waited, looking around. As well as several storerooms, and the main hall in which a small team of volunteers was busy sorting out the bags of donated items, Kate could see what looked like some sort of lounge, with sofas and bean-bags and a bookcase. As she looked, the sound of footsteps echoed behind her and a soft voice said, "I'm Ruth Granger, the manager here. How can I help?"

Ruth Granger led them to the little sitting room that Kate had glimpsed and shut the door. She gestured for the officers to sit down and they did so. Kate realised that all the furniture in here was shabby, and the books in the bookcase were all rather dog-eared, the few magazines on the coffee table a couple of months out of date. Nonetheless, it was still rather a cosy room and gave the impression of someone trying to do the best they could with what little they had.

"I thought we'd better have some privacy," Ruth said as she seated herself on a battered leather pouffe.

She looked to be about thirty-five, with a thin pretty face but a truly arresting mane of totally grey hair. Kate, who had pulled the fifteenth grey hair from her scalp that very morning, was impressed with someone so young who was obviously happy to look as nature intended. It even looked rather good; a striking contrast to Ruth's still youthful face.

Ruth was still speaking with a serious look on her face. "We have refugees coming in all the time and a lot of them—well, they'd be seriously alarmed to see police here. Not just because some of them are here—well, illegally—but you can imagine, the places that they've come from, the police are...feared."

"I understand," said Olbeck.

Ruth went on. "Some of what we do is teaching them about the different culture here, about how the police can help you and are not to be feared."

"I'm relieved to hear that," Olbeck said with a smile. "I'm sure you do a lot of good."

Ruth inclined her grey head, modestly. "Well, we try to. God knows, there's a need for it. I used to run the refugee solidarity group here, and we were overwhelmed with stuff that needed to be done. It was like a gift from heaven when Sanctuary decided to take over."

"When was that, exactly?"

"About six months ago. Of course, there's still a lot of work to be done..." She trailed off, glancing about the room. Kate saw the shadow of a frown on her face.

Olbeck drew out the photograph of the dead man but kept it face down. "We're hoping you might be able to help us with an identification, Ms Granger. You might have heard about a body that was found on a beach near here, Muddiford Beach?"

Ruth nodded, her eyes wide. "Yes, I did read something about that in the papers."

Olbeck continued. "Well, we're still trying to identify the body, and we have reason to believe that he may have been a migrant or a refugee. Would you be able to take a look at this picture and see if you recognise him?" Ruth reached out for the photograph he was proffering, still face-down, and he added, hastily, "I should tell you that that is a post-mortem photograph. I'm sorry, but it's the only one we have of him currently."

Ruth had recoiled upon the words 'post-mortem'. Then she reached out again for the photograph, with slightly shaking fingers, and turned it right side up.

She had clearly braced herself for what she was going to see, and Kate saw her let her held breath out in a sigh. Her face flickered. "No," she said, after a moment. "I'm afraid I have no idea who this is."

"None whatsoever?" asked Kate.

Ruth was still looking at the dead man's face, frowning now. "I don't recognise him but—" Both Kate and Olbeck leaned forward in anticipation. "There's something..." She was biting her lip now, obviously thinking hard. She looked at the police officers. "I can't say I recognise him—I mean, I have no idea of his name or anything but—it's odd—there's something, just a flicker of familiarity about him. I'm sorry, I'm not being clear. Perhaps he just reminds me of someone else I know. Sorry."

Kate felt a surge of frustration. For a second there, she thought they might actually be getting somewhere.

Ruth was still looking at the photograph. After a moment, she handed it back to Olbeck, still frowning. "I'm sorry I can't help you."

"Never mind," Olbeck said neutrally. He and Kate got up and handed over their cards. "If you do remember anything, please do get in touch."

"Yes, of course." Ruth showed them to the door of the sitting room.

"Would you mind if we ran this past your volunteers?" Kate asked, somewhat pointlessly because she and Olbeck were going to do just that, permission or no permission. But it never hurt to be polite.

"Yes, of course," Ruth said again, ushering them towards the main hall. "But I'm not sure they'll be able to help. This team are all new, they've only been volunteering for a few days."

True to Ruth's word, none of the five volunteers could identify the man, although their reactions to the photograph ranged from quiet disgust to semi-hysterical shrieks from one teenager with a gold ring through her nose. Kate and Olbeck thanked them, thanked Ruth Granger, and took their leave.

As they left the building, they passed a young woman, dressed in a modest long skirt, with a headscarf covering her hair. She eyed them almost fearfully as they passed before dropping her gaze hastily, as if the sight of Kate and Olbeck had burned her. Even as Kate turned a little to watch her, the woman—girl, really, she couldn't have been more than twenty-five—scurried into the building as fast as she could. Kate mentally shrugged. Could that woman have been one of the traumatised refugees that Ruth Granger had mentioned? One of the ones for whom the police would always be something to fear? Kate and Olbeck were plainclothes, as were all detectives, but perhaps a refugee who'd grown up in a repressively-policed state could detect officers even if they weren't in uniform.

"So, what do you think?" Kate asked, once they were back in the car and driving away. "Think Ruth was telling us the truth?"

"Oh, I think so," said Olbeck. "If not, she's a very accomplished actress. No, I think she might have seen him somewhere but not know who he is. I hope she remembers."

"We should have left the photograph," said Kate. "With our numbers on the bottom of it. Someone might recognise him."

Olbeck gave her a disbelieving look. "Kate, you can't pin a picture of a *dead body* on the noticeboard of a refugee crisis centre. Can you imagine how triggering that would be to these poor people, especially after what they've been through?"

"Oh yes," Kate said, chastened. She was quiet for a moment and then said "Mind you, once Sam does his computer thingy for the press, we could get some posters made and pin them up, couldn't we? Once he doesn't look quite so dead, I mean."

Olbeck shrugged. "I suppose we might have to, if we can't get hold of anything else to use."

They drove in silence for a few minutes. Kate was trying to think of what to do next. "Have we run a DNA match yet?"

"I think Rav is sorting that one out." Olbeck indicated to turn right, taking the main road back to Abbeyford. "That's if Salterton haven't taken that over. God, I'm not really a fan of joint investigations, I'll tell you that."

"You don't need to tell *me*," said Kate. "You don't have to work with *Mein Kommandant* Chloe Wapping, for a start. Count yourself lucky."

When Kate got home that night, darkness had already fallen. The gentle warmth of the day had long since dissipated, and Kate shivered as she switched off the car headlights, turned off the engine and, grabbing her bag, got out of the car. Pushing open the garden gate, she had the shock of her life as a dark figure moved towards her from the front door.

"Bloody hell!"

"Sorry," said Tin. "I thought you could see it was me. You really need to get that outside light fixed, Kate."

Kate stood clutching her chest. "You scared the hell out of me." She had a piercing flash of memory: stood here, saying just the same thing to her brother Jay, years ago. She hadn't changed the bulb in the outside light since that day, she realised, with a slightly guilty pang.

"Sorry," Tin said again. "But you haven't been returning my texts. I wanted to see you."

"The fact that I haven't texted you back should be a bit of a warning that I don't want to see *you* at the moment," Kate said, pulling herself together.

"Well, it was either this or I would have been forced to hold another sign up outside your office window," Tin said with a smile, and Kate found herself laughing despite herself.

"Oh, come on in, then. It's too cold to hang around out here."

Once inside, Kate checked the heating was on, switched on the lamps in the sitting room, drew the curtains against the cold blackness of the windows and put a match to the fire that she'd laid that morning before leaving for work. Despite her annoyance with what Tin had done at the crime scene, she couldn't help but be pleased to see him. The magic of her own home was working on her too—the sense of calm and comfort that all her familiar things induced in her.

Since the incident earlier in the year, when Kate had fought off a killer in this very room, she'd repainted and re-carpeted and bought a new sofa and armchair, performing a kind of exorcism. It had worked too— there were very few bad memories left.

"Don't expect me to cook," she said, still not quite willing to unbend completely.

"Don't worry, I wasn't. I'll order us a takeaway."

He'd brought wine too, and Kate thought she might have one glass with her meal. Despite a period of fairly heavy drinking, during the time she was grieving for her mother, Kate had since reverted to her almost-teetotal ways. But one drink, now and again, could be enjoyable. She plopped down on the sofa and stretched her socked feet out to the strengthening flames in the grate.

"So, anyway," Tin said, coming back into the room with two full glasses. "Again, I wanted to say sorry about surprising you at the beach the other day. It was stupid and crass of me."

"Yes, it was," agreed Kate. She took an appreciative sip of the wine in her glass.

"I'm quite surprised we haven't had to deal with that sort of situation before."

Kate had also found herself thinking the same thing. "You know I can't possibly discuss anything about the case with you," she said sternly.

"Yeah, I know. That's not to say that I might not be able to help you, though,"

Kate eyed him above the rim of her glass. "In what way?"

Tin relaxed back into the sofa cushions, holding his own wine glass. "Well, who's to say that I might not be able to find out who this guy is?"

Kate sat up. "Do you know?"

Tin looked a bit sheepish. "No, actually I don't. But that's not to say I couldn't find out."

Kate sat back again. "Okay. If you find out anything that might help the investigation then obviously report it. But *not* to me. Ring the station number and talk to them." Tin nodded. "And now I think this part of the conversation should finish," Kate added.

Tin nodded again. "I quite agree." He leant forward and took the glass from Kate's hands, putting it next to his own on the coffee table. Then he gently drew Kate towards him. "Besides, who wants to *talk* all evening?"

"What about the takeaway?" asked Kate between kisses, breathless already.

Tin grinned. "We'll work up an appetite."

Chapter Seven

AS SHE DROVE TO THE office the next morning, Kate found herself thinking about what Ruth Granger had told them. She walked into the office so deep in thought that she almost ran into Theo, who was walking back to his desk with a full mug of coffee.

"Jesus, woman!" He made a complicated body move to avoid coffee slopping onto his expensive suit. "Watch where you're going. You're away with the fairies, this morning."

"Oh, sorry." Kate ran for some paper napkins to mop up the spill on the carpet. Once that was under control, she recollected herself and headed for her desk, firing up her computer.

Theo was still fussing and tutting, over by his own desk. She could hear him grumbling something about Oswald Boateng and, after a moment, called over, "Well, what do you expect when you wear expensive stuff to work?"

Theo gave her a look. "You're lucky I don't land you with the dry-cleaning bill."

"I *said* I'm sorry. Why don't you just wear something a bit less...fancy?"

Theo scoffed and adjusted his cuffs. "Because, Kate, some of us, unlike you, like to look good at work."

Kate debated spilling something else over him but decided against it. After a moment, Theo came over to her desk. "Right, now that you've baptised me, perhaps we can start getting some work done? How did you and Mark get on yesterday with the refugee centre?"

Kate shook her head. "No dice. Although—" She recollected Ruth Granger's hesitation once more. "I might have a quick look at the charity that runs it. Sanctuary. Just to get a bit of background info."

"Knock yourself out," said Theo. "I met one of the founders once. Nuria Sanderby."

"'Nuria Sanderby'?" Kate asked, wondering who he was talking about. She tried to remember if she knew anything about her—it was a fairly distinctive name, after all—and after a moment, a faint recollection of a rather striking dark woman who dressed in white came back to her.

"Yeah, her. She was cool. Seriously hot, even if she is a little bit out of my age range."

Kate rolled her eyes, wondering why she was even bothering with this. "And how did you meet this goddess?"

"Charity fundraiser in London. My mother had tickets."

"Nuria Sanderby is one of the founders of Sanctuary?" Kate asked, just to be sure.

"Yeah. Her and her husband. She was an asylum seeker herself, years ago, and then they set up this charity to help the refugees a couple of years ago. Raised tons of money. Her husband's some sort of posh dude. They've done tons of fundraising."

"Right," said Kate. She turned to her computer, thinking she might as well do a bit of research. Theo wandered back to his own desk after a moment.

Kate soon found the charity's website and spent the next hour reading it. Theo had been right—the founders of the charity were Nuria Sanderby and her husband, Peregrine Sanderby. *Peregrine*... Kate permitted herself a quiet chuckle at the name. Imagine going through school with a name like that...although he'd probably gone to Eton or somewhere like that, where those sort of names were three a penny (Kate imagined). She looked keenly at the many pictures on the site. Nuria Sanderby seemed to always dress in white—it suited her striking, dark looks. Her husband was more flamboyant, in various brightly coloured and thickly embroidered waistcoats with a mane of greyish-blonde hair, rather longer than you were used to seeing on a man in his fifties.

Kate read through all the text that detailed their charity fundraising efforts. There were some impressive celebrity names associated with the charity. Kate was amused to see that one of the less impressive ones was Casey Bright, someone Kate had encountered in her very first case in Abbeyford.

Casey had gone through several husbands, since her divorce from Nick Fullman, and was apparently now married to a rock musician who was also a patron of the charity.

After another twenty minutes, Kate came to the conclusion that there were probably better ways to spend her time. Should she go through the thick pile of forensic reports that had arrived that morning? Pondering, she made herself and Theo a coffee ("Mind the suit!" he'd yelped as she handed it over and she'd stuck her tongue out at him) and went back to her desk. The post mortem report from Andrew was the top file on the pile of cardboard folders on her desk. Kate opened it and sat down to read.

Several post mortem photographs of the dead man were uppermost in the file. Kate looked at them, noting that, even in death, he had a handsome face. She felt a spasm of pity for him, so young, his whole life ahead of him...and then someone had ripped it away from him and there was nothing, a blank, a dead-end of a future. Why had they done it? What was the motive? Kate tapped a pen against the side of her jaw, thinking. Robbery? It seemed unlikely, given his air of poverty. An argument? Over what?

Blowing out her cheeks, she sat back in her chair and her eyes went to her computer screen. Then she gasped.

"Oh, my God." Kate leant forward, looking from the photograph on the website to the post mortem photograph on the desk before her. Then back again. Her eyes scanned the computer screen so closely she almost pressed her nose up against the screen. Then she sat back again, clasping her hands.

"Theo," she said, trying to keep her voice calm. "Come over here a minute, would you?"

He ambled over. "What's up?"

Kate pointed at the photograph on the website. "Look. There. And now, look here." She moved her finger to rest on the photograph of the dead man's face.

Theo swore. "It looks like him."

"It *is* him. I'm almost sure of it."

Theo began hurriedly reading the text that bordered the photograph on the computer screen. "There's no name. Is there?"

Kate looked again at the screen. The photograph that had drawn their attention was of the Sanderbys, on some kind of outdoor stage, addressing a crowd, at some sort of event or rally. Kate thought she recognised the backdrop of Hyde Park, in London—you could see the edge of the memorial to Prince Albert in one corner of the photograph. There were others on the stage with the Sanderbys, and whomever the dead man had been, he appeared to be one of them. He was standing three people away from Nuria Sanderby, his face serious, with his hands folded in front of him.

"If it is him," said Theo, "then they know him. Don't they?"

"I don't know," said Kate. "We don't know anything

about him. We've got to make sure it is him before we start doing anything."

"Yeah, I know. Get IT to get some facial recognition experts in, they can do a point by point match of the two photographs."

Kate was already reaching for the phone. "Actually, we'll still need to interview the Sanderbys anyway. They might be able to tell us who he is straight away."

"Run it past the boss," Theo said. "And then we'll get going."

"Kate," Anderton greeted her amiably as she knocked on his half-open door. "What's the problem?"

"There's no problem," said Kate, finding a chair to sit down on. "We've got a potential match for our beach body victim."

Anderton's eyebrows rose. "Oh, yes?"

Kate qualified her statement a little. "Well, we've discovered a couple of people who might be able to identify him for us. The Sanderbys, the ones who run the refugee charity, Sanctuary."

"Oh, it's that one, is it? They've been in the papers a fair few times, haven't they?" Anderton rubbed his chin, pondering. "I may have even made them a donation myself, come to think of it."

"Really?"

"I've got a few charities I support, and once we started hearing all these dreadful stories about the war in Syria, and all the drownings in Europe and what-have-you, well, you want to be able to help, don't you? Even if it is just giving some money."

Kate nodded. "So, Theo and I can head up there today if that's okay with you? See if we can get an immediate identification."

Anderton looked sceptical. "Well, give it a go." Kate thanked him and got up out of her seat. "Hold on a minute. What about your Salterton colleague?"

Kate stopped halfway to the door. It would be fair to say that so far, that morning, she'd almost forgotten the existence of Chloe Wapping. She groaned inwardly at the remembrance.

Anderton looked as though he could read her mind. "It's only fair to let her know what you've discovered, don't you think?"

Kate sagged a little. Then she straightened up. "Yes, I suppose so." She began walking towards his office door again.

"Wait a moment." Anderton's voice stopped her forward motion. "Sit down, for a sec, and shut the door."

Kate did as she was instructed. She felt a flicker of nervousness as she sat back down in her chair. For several months now, she'd quite successfully avoided being alone with Anderton, something she thought would be a wise move, given the odd attraction that seemed to wax and wane between them. It made her uncomfortable to think about it, and she tended to shove the thoughts away when they occurred. She and Anderton had shared a kiss, about six months ago, not to mention their one-night-stand all those years ago. At the time of the kiss, things had been very new with Tin and she hadn't mentioned it, although she was still stabbed with guilt now and again. Now, as things seemed to be getting more serious between Tin and herself, it made it even more crucial that the sexual attraction between herself and her boss was kept under control. Easier said than done, thought Kate with an inner sigh, making herself concentrate on what Anderton was saying.

"I know it's difficult when you have to work with people you're not used to working with. Even more so when it's a totally different station, team, culture— you know the sort of thing." Anderton had got up and was attempting to pace around his office, without much success; it was just too small and crowded. He came to rest at the window, resting his hands on the sill and staring out at the rooftops of Abbeyford. "It's especially difficult when you have a bit of a personality clash."

Had Olbeck mentioned something? Kate wondered. "I'm not quite sure what you mean—" she began, but he talked over her.

"It's been mentioned that you and DS Wapping are— perhaps—somewhat antagonistic towards one another."

Olbeck *had* said something, then. The git. "Well, she's hardly the most likeable person, to be honest, sir. Though, I dare say, it's as much my fault as hers."

Anderton turned around to face her, leaning back

against the windowsill. "You can be incredibly hard on other women, Kate. Have you ever noticed that?"

Kate stared at him. "What do you mean?" she asked, once she'd recovered her voice.

Anderton shrugged. "Just that. You're hard on other women, sometimes. You're less patient, you're more intolerant than you are with your male colleagues, I've noticed."

Kate was flabbergasted. "I am not! I get on perfectly well with—" For a moment, she couldn't recall a single name. "I worked perfectly well with Jane, when she was here."

Anderton was watching her keenly. "What about Fliss?" he asked, naming an ex-colleague.

"She tried to kill me!"

"Ah, well," Anderton said, in what Kate felt was an unnecessarily reasonable voice. "There was that, yes."

Kate was silent for a moment, shaken. Was it true? Did she treat her female colleagues differently to her male ones? More importantly, if indeed she did treat other women differently, was she treating them *worse*? What a hypocrite, if so... Kate thought of all the struggles she'd had through her career; being patronised, being belittled, the outright sexism and discrimination that she'd faced or become aware of... What if she was contributing to that? It was a dreadful thought, so bad that she was tempted to reject it outright.

Why was Anderton telling her this now? She had a

moment's thought that perhaps he enjoyed upsetting her, that he got some sort of kick out of seeing her lose her temper. The thought made her grit her teeth. Was it true? Was that his way of coping with his feelings towards her, whereas she coped with hers by pretending that they (and sometimes he) didn't exist?

Her head whirling, Kate realised she'd been silent for too long. She looked up and forced a smile. "That's an interesting thought, sir. I'll take it on board." It cost her some effort to say just that, in an even tone of voice, but she felt better for doing so afterwards.

Anderton looked at her sympathetically and, for a moment, Kate was ashamed of the mental accusations she'd just made towards him. I'm being paranoid, she told herself.

Anderton pushed himself upright from the window. "We seem to have got a bit side-tracked, haven't we?"

"Wouldn't be the first time," Kate was unable to help muttering under her breath. Aghast at her own daring, she waited for Anderton's response but she wasn't sure he'd heard.

She thought she heard him chuckle faintly as he sat back down. Certainly he was smiling as he looked across at her. "All I'm saying, Kate, is that everyone has their stories. And for other women in the force, don't you think that they might have gone through some of the same struggles and pressure as you?"

"Maybe," Kate said reluctantly.

"It might help to regard DS Wapping as an ally, that's all. Rather than an enemy."

There was a lot Kate wanted to say to that, but marshalling all the contradictory thoughts in her head and voicing them in the right order would have taken more mental energy that she was capable of at the moment. She contented herself with nodding and saying again, "I'll definitely take it on board, sir."

"Oh, less of the 'sir'," said Anderton, reaching for a folder on his desk. His gaze met Kate's, and something of the tension in the air was broken. "Make sure you report back to me as soon as you think you might have something."

"Of course," Kate said smartly. "Goodbye." She got up and left his office, shutting the door behind her, and walked back to her desk with her head in a whirl.

Chapter Eight

KATE AND THEO WERE WALKING towards Kate's car when Kate found her footsteps slowing.

"What's up?" Theo looked over at her enquiringly.

Kate bit her lip. "Just something the boss said. Do you think we should let Salterton know what we're up to?"

Theo snorted. "There's no point telling that fat git I've got to work with anything. He's the laziest bastard I've ever come across."

Kate wasn't even sure which officer from Salterton Theo had been paired with. "All the same," she said, reluctantly. "Maybe I should inform DS Wapping that we've got a lead."

"Well, if you must..." Theo trailed off as Kate reached for her phone. "Hang on a minute, though. If she wants to come, that makes three of us. It doesn't need that many of us."

"Shall I check?"

"Yes, check. And if Chloe Whatsit does want to

come, I'm going to bow out. I've got tons of stuff to do otherwise."

"Okay." Kate called up Chloe's mobile number on her phone, inwardly groaning. Why couldn't Anderton just have kept his thoughts to himself? Kate would have blithely gone up to London with Theo, and whilst he could be a cocky little bugger, his company was infinitely preferable to bloody Chloe Wapping's... Kate heard the line ringing and prayed that Chloe wouldn't answer it.

"DS Wapping." Boy, she sounded about as welcoming as an executioner. Obviously Kate's name had come up with her number on Chloe's phone.

"Hi—it's DS Redman—"

"I know. What do you want?"

Charming. "I just wanted to let you know that we might have a lead we're pursuing." Kate went on to explain exactly what she'd found and what she and Theo had intended to do. "We were wondering whether you might like to come along with us," she ended, rather lamely.

There was a silence on the end of the line. Then Chloe said in a guarded voice, "That sort of interview wouldn't need three of us."

Precisely what Theo had pointed out. Kate thought again of what Anderton had said, his parting words to her particularly, and asked, "I thought perhaps you and I could go and interview the Sanderbys."

She held her breath. Then Chloe said in a somewhat

friendlier tone, "Yes. Yes, okay." There was another silence and Kate was about to start suggesting travel arrangements but Chloe added abruptly, "Thank you."

"It's no problem," Kate said hastily. "If you're at Salterton now, I'll come and pick you up in twenty minutes or so."

"Yes. Yes, I am here. I'll—I'll wait for you, then."

"Okay, great." Kate said goodbye and hung up. She felt a moment of trepidation at the thought of being trapped in a car with Chloe for a couple of hours on the way to London. At least there was always the radio...

"All good?" Theo asked. "She's coming?"

"Yep."

"Good. I can get on with things here, then. I'll get the photo ID in motion."

"Thanks," Kate said, gratefully. Even if the interview with the Sanderbys proved fruitless, at least with technology they might be able to match the body and the photograph, and that was one step closer to a positive identification.

Early afternoon was a good time to hit the motorway. The bulk of the morning traffic had thinned out and it was still too early for the evening rush hour to begin. Kate found she was making good time to the capital and the easy drive meant she could devote some more brain space to the questions she was going to ask the Sanderbys.

Being with Chloe wasn't quite as awkward as

she'd anticipated. It helped that Chloe had greeted her quite pleasantly, for a change, and that for the majority of the journey, Chloe had been glued to her mobile, relieving Kate of the necessity to make small talk. After a while, she realised Chloe was viewing the Sanctuary website on her smartphone.

"You have a good eye, DS Redman," was the first thing that she'd said for nearly an hour.

"Sorry?" Kate looked over at her, startled.

"To make the identification from that picture. It's not as if you've got a large image to go from." Kate wondered for a second if she was taking the piss and her eyes narrowed but after a moment, Chloe went on in an approving tone. "It would have been easy to miss."

Kate relaxed a little. "Well, it was probably also the fact that I had his picture from the PM there right in front of me. If I hadn't, perhaps I wouldn't have noticed. The conditions for spotting the resemblance were right."

"Well, let's hope this visit gives us something concrete to work with." Chloe sounded more amiable than she had done at any time before.

Kate drove for a moment, thinking. Then, taking advantage of the more relaxed mood in the car, she asked a tentative question. "So, what made you join the police?"

A mistake. As soon as she'd asked it, the easier

atmosphere changed. She could see the chill settling back into Chloe's features.

"I don't really remember," Chloe said, after a moment. Her tone was distant.

Kate flexed her fingers on the steering wheel. Part of her was thinking, fuck it, why should I make the effort when she's not going to? The other part of her was remembering Anderton's words. *And for other women in the force, don't you think that they might have gone through the same struggles and pressure as you?* Kate took a deep breath and made the metaphorical leap.

"I didn't have a great childhood," she said, almost surprising herself. No less Chloe, who was clearly startled into looking straight at her. "I'm just mentioning that because it's relevant to why *I* joined the police."

There was a silence and Kate braced herself for a sarcastic comment. "Why are you telling me this?" or "So why would you think I care?" Something of that nature. Instead Chloe asked "So, why did you join the police then?"

Kate risked a glance sideways. Chloe wasn't sneering—she looked puzzled, but not hostile. "I had so much chaos in my childhood, the one thing I really wanted was order. Joining the police felt like...relief."

She'd said a bit more than she intended to and cringed a little. She could just see Chloe throwing that titbit back in her face at some point. But the other woman said nothing and looked thoughtful. After a moment, Chloe said, "It felt a bit like that for me, too."

That was the closest Kate had so far got to an emotional connection with her Salterton colleague. Some sixth sense warned her not to push it, not to enquire further. Instead, she made a noise of agreement and turned her attention back to the road. She pictured Anderton in her mind's eye and thought he would be pleased with her. A tiny step, perhaps, but a step forward nonetheless.

The Sanctuary offices were something of a surprise. Kate had visited many charities before and apart from the really big ones—the internationally known ones— most were housed in fairly basic accommodation. The head offices of Sanctuary were in an Art Deco building just on the edge of Crystal Palace, in South London. The house itself was quite striking: a stark white box with a characteristic flat roof, metal-framed windows and stylised 1920s designs adorning the front door and windows. It looked more like a private residence than a charity head office, and Kate, pulling up on the gravel sweep of the driveway, wondered whether it was, in fact, the Sanderbys' home as well as their place of work.

Kate had rung ahead and ascertained that both the Sanderbys would be present that afternoon—a relief, as she'd not wanted to risk a long drive to London without being sure that the interview would definitely go ahead. As she gathered together her coat and bag, she could see Chloe observing the exterior of the house and wondered what her thoughts were. There was no time to ask now—she could see someone walking towards them.

The woman approaching them was tall and slim and striking, quite beautiful in a patrician looking way. She was dressed from top to toe in white: linen trousers, a white tunic, white canvas plimsolls, a white flower pinned in the curls of her long, dark hair. As she came nearer, Kate realised it was a real flower, a white rose-bud, the petals coiled in amongst themselves, damp and creamy looking.

"You must be the police," the woman said. She had a low, attractive voice, the hint of her foreign origins still apparent. Kate had already guessed who she was but the woman went on to confirm it. "I'm Nuria Sanderby. Do come in and meet my husband. I hope we can be of assistance."

"I hope so too, Mrs Sanderby," Kate said, shaking the woman's hand. She introduced Chloe. "It's good of you to see us so promptly."

By now, they were being ushered inside the hallway. Inside, the house was as striking as the exterior, and Kate commented favourably on the original Art Deco features such as the lovely parquet flooring and the slanting handles of the doors.

"Must cost a fortune to run," Chloe said abruptly,

the first time she had spoken. "Even in this part of London."

Nuria Sanderby looked at her with surprise, and Kate couldn't exactly blame her. "Oh, the actual house is part of my husband's estate," she said diffidently, showing them through into a room off of the hallway, which turned out to be an office. There was an actual fire burning in the original fireplace, over on the outside wall, and it made the whole room at once wonderfully cosy. A tall, thin man was stood with his back to the fire, an unlit pipe in the corner of his mouth, rocking back and forth a little on the soles of his feet. He was dressed quite as eccentrically as his wife although displaying a lot more colour. His trousers looked as though they were made of some sort of orange silk and he wore a waistcoat that was thickly embroidered with gold and coloured thread.

"My husband, Peregrine Sanderby," introduced Nuria. Sanderby came forward to shake the hands of both of the police officers.

"Charmed to meet you both. This is a bit of a to-do, isn't it? We're at a bit of a loss to see how we can help, but we'll both do our best, I'm sure. Now, can I offer you two charming ladies a drink of something? Something hot? Something cold? Do you still not drink on duty or was that just always a myth?"

Swamped with charm and questions, Kate could feel a giggle building up in her throat. She cleared it, without daring to look over at Chloe to see how she was taking it. "Nothing for me, thank you Mr Sanderby."

"Perry, please. Do call me Perry, everyone does. Well, it's not surprising, is it, having been saddled with a name like *Peregrine*. What on Earth my parents were thinking, I don't know." He beamed at them, and Kate smiled back, her own thoughts on his eccentric name uppermost. "Now, if I can't get either of you a drink, what can we do for you?"

Before Kate could open her mouth, Chloe stepped forward. "We need you to tell us if you can identify a victim of a crime."

The Sanderbys exchanged glances.

"What... what kind of crime?" asked Peregrine, tentatively.

"Murder."

Nuria Sanderby gave a faint gasp. Kate, annoyed with her colleague, moved to explain. She told the Sanderbys about the body of the young man found on the beach and about how they'd matched his picture to the man seen in the photograph of the Sanderbys at the refugee rally.

"Oh, of course I know what you mean," cried Nuria, sounding distressed. "But I thought—wasn't the body an asylum seeker, a refugee who'd been trying to reach England? I thought he was supposed to have drowned, poor man."

Kate saw Peregrine reach for her hand and gently squeeze it. "That's unfortunately not the case,

Mrs Sanderby. Some of the earlier media reports were inaccurate."

"I see." Nuria looked down at the floor. Kate could see the sparkle of tears at the edge of her dark eyelashes.

"We believe the man found dead on Muddiford Beach in Somerset is the same man who has been pictured with you in one of the photographs on your website," Kate said. "We need you to have a look at his picture and see if you can identify him."

"Well, of course," said Peregrine, sounding troubled. "The poor chap. Do you have the photograph?"

Chloe thrust it forward rather abruptly. Nuria reached out a long hand, thin fingers encircled with many glittering rings, and took it. She seemed to brace herself before she looked at the picture.

Kate saw Nuria let out a little huff of surprise when she raised the photograph to her gaze. She opened her mouth to say something but Nuria was already speaking, rather breathlessly. "Yes, I do know him. I *do*. Oh, what was his name?" She shook the picture at her husband. "Look, Perry, look, it's that young man—oh, what was his *name*?"

"So you *do* know him?" asked Kate, feeling a leap of excitement.

Nuria nodded. The trembling tears on the edge of her eyelids overflowed and ran down her face. She wiped at her cheeks with her free hand. "Yes, I do recognise him. He was an Eritrean refugee, he spoke about his experiences at the rally. Gayle organised it, he was one of the key speakers, after us..." Who was Gayle? Kate tried to marshal her thoughts, and decide what to ask first, but Nuria rushed on. "Gayle might even have his contact details. I just wish I could remember his *name*."

Peregrine was still staring at the photograph of the dead man. "I *think* his name was Ali," he said, almost absently. "I can't remember his surname. Gayle would know." Before Kate or Chloe could ask who Gayle was, Peregrine strode over to the door, opened and bellowed "Gayle? Gayle! Come in here for a moment, would you?"

Gayle Templeton turned out to be a personal assistant to both the Sanderbys. She was a short, slim woman with very pale blue eyes and coppery coloured hair cut into a short, sharp bob, rather appropriate for the 1920s setting of the office. Kate had the impression that she prided herself on appearing cool and unruffled next to the more expressive, Bohemian personalities of her employers.

When presented with the photograph of the dead man, she looked at it with calm indifference. "Yes, I know exactly who that is. His name is Ali Araya. He was one of the speakers that day, I'd organised for him to attend."

"How did you meet him?" asked Kate.

The cold blue eyes met hers with no sign of anxiety. "I contacted our shelter managers to see if there were any refugees who would be happy to speak at the rally."

"So, Ali was—what—recommended to you as someone who would speak?"

"That's right. I had his name put forward by Ruth Granger, the manager at our Salterton centre."

"Ruth Granger?" Kate checked. "You're sure about that?"

"Yes," said Gayle, calmly.

Kate's gaze went almost instinctively to meet Chloe's. If Gayle was telling the truth, then why had Ruth not recognised the photograph of Ali immediately, if she'd known him well enough to suggest he might speak at one of Sanctuary's rallies?

Nuria had sunk onto a leather desk chair and had put her head in her hands. Peregrine stood beside her, patting her rather awkwardly on the shoulder.

"I can't bear it," Nuria said, her voice low and ragged with tears. "I remember him well. Poor Ali. He'd gone through so much to get here, he'd suffered so much and then for this to happen, just as he was starting afresh..."

"Did you know him well?" asked Kate, moving a little closer.

Nuria sat up, wiping her face. Kate had expected to see mascara streaked in black rivelets under her eyes but clearly, those were Nuria's real eyelashes, unadorned with make-up. She shook her head. "No. No, I didn't know him well. Well, *we* didn't."

She glanced up at Peregrine. "I just remember him speaking at the rally. He made a very good speech. It was very affecting."

Peregrine removed his hand from his wife's shoulder and clasped it with his other hand behind his back. He began a slow rocking back and forth, rising to the balls or his feet and then sinking back in an almost meditative manner. "He spoke about coming over on a boat to Greece. He said it was so overloaded it was swaying in the water. When they got within sight of land—they were heading for an island, I can't remember the name offhand—the crew started throwing the children overboard." He looked at Kate, a haunted expression on his face. "They were wearing life jackets but they were too big for them and they slipped out and under the water. Ali said the mothers were screaming but they couldn't get to the windows to climb out to reach their children."

There was silence in the room for a moment. "Oh my god, that's awful," said Kate inadequately.

Peregrine half smiled. "It actually had a happy ending, his story, believe it or not. Some English ladies were on the beach, they were on holiday and they saw what was happening and swam out. All the children were rescued. Ali said he saw one tiny boy clinging round the neck of one of the ladies for dear life. Even when she got him to the shore, he wouldn't let go."

The fire crackled in the silence that fell. Kate tried

to block out the images the anecdote had conjured in her brain and bring herself back to the present. "So—so, that was your only contact with Ali, at the rally?" she asked, after a moment.

Nuria wiped the corner of her eyes with a long, thin finger. "I think so. Wait—Perry, did we meet him when we were in Salterton in June? I'm trying to think..." They all waited for her to speak again. Eventually she did. "I think we may have met him at the centre. We were making one of our monthly visits, and I'm almost sure that we were at least introduced. Or was that earlier?"

Peregrine didn't confirm or contradict her assertion. He made a shrugging motion with his shoulders, his mouth quirked in an 'I'm not sure' kind of grimace.

Kate waited but Nuria seemed to have stopped speaking. She looked over at Chloe, wondering if her colleague wanted to ask any questions, but Chloe was looking over at the fire with a fierce sort of concentration.

"We'll need a statement from all three of you with regards to your meeting or meetings with Ali Araya and for anything you can tell us about him," Kate said.

Nuria and Peregrine nodded, looking serious. Gayle gave her a quick smile that was somehow dismissive.

Chloe spoke up into the silence that followed Kate's request. "We'll also need to know your whereabouts between the hours of eleven pm and four am on the second of October."

"Our whereabouts?" Nuria said blankly.

"Yes." Chloe looked her directly in the face.

Nuria looked nervous. "I see. Was that... Was that when—"

"Just tell me where you were."

Kate hastened to add something. "It's standard procedure, that's all."

Both Nuria and Peregrine looked over at Gayle. She went over to a desk and picked up a leather-bound diary.

"What was the date?" she asked coolly.

"The second of October."

Gayle flicked over a page. "Oh yes. The fundraising dinner at the Savoy." She looked up at the police officers. "Both Mr and Mrs Sanderby were at a charity event until midnight that evening."

"At the Savoy Hotel?" Kate checked.

"Yes, that's correct."

"She's a marvel," Peregrine said confidingly to Kate. "Keeps us all together, always knows where we're supposed to be and what we're supposed to be doing."

Kate looked over to see how Gayle had taken that but the other woman was looking quite blank-faced. After a moment, she smiled a smile that didn't quite reach those cold blue eyes.

Kate and Chloe handed over their cards. As they

began their goodbyes, Nuria put a hand out to stop Kate as she went to pick up the photo of Ali Araya.

"It seems so cruel," Nuria said softly. She was looking at his face, handsome even in death, the closed eyes. Kate nodded. Nuria took one more look and then picked up the photograph to hand it back. Kate could see the sparkle of tears once more in her eyes and wondered if she, like Kate, was thinking of the cruel irony; to have survived a perilous sea crossing only to die on a beach of the country that had taken you in.

Chapter Nine

"WHAT DO YOU KNOW ABOUT Eritrea?" Kate asked Olbeck, the next morning, as she carried a cup of tea over to his desk.

Olbeck looked up in anticipation of his first hot drink of the day. "Ooh, lovely. What was that? What do I know of Eritrea?" He took an appreciative sip. "Bugger all. It's in Africa, isn't it?"

"It's where our murder victim originally came from," said Kate. "According to his asylum claim, Ali Araya left Eritrea about eighteen months before he arrived in the UK, in February of this year."

"Right," said Olbeck, gulping his tea down.

Kate flipped open the notebook she held in one hand. "Apparently Eritrea has one of the most repressive governments on the planet. It's sometimes known as the 'North Korea of Africa', and its citizens are routinely subjected to imprisonment, beatings and torture."

"Well, you can see why the poor bugger wanted to leave then, can't you?" Olbeck said. He put his

CELINA GRACE

empty mug down and almost immediately jumped up. "Come on, this morning is definitely a two-cup morning. Let's get another drink."

They made their way over to where the kettle and mugs were kept, Kate informing Olbeck of random facts about Eritrea along the way.

"I suppose we should see if we can contact his family," Olbeck said, flipping the switch of the kettle down. "If he had a family, of course. God, I'm not even sure where we would start, if what you're telling me is true. It sounds like a bloody awful place."

"Yes, I know," said Kate, glancing at her notes. "Makes you wonder why they're not all headed over here."

"God forbid," said Rav, who had obviously overhead what they were talking about. He got up from his desk to join them. "Besides," he added darkly, "they're not all from Eritrea."

"Who aren't?" asked Kate.

"All those refugees," said Rav. Then he made quote marks in the air. "Or 'refugees', as I might call them. Yeah, right."

"Rav!" said Kate, shocked by his tone. "What do you mean?"

"Come on, Kate, they're not all fleeing persecution, are they? Most of them are young men—they're *economic migrants*, not refugees. They just want to come over here because we let them, because they can get a better quality of life over here and not even have to pay for it."

88

Kate was open-mouthed by this time. "Rav, what on Earth are you saying? Besides, weren't *your* parents immigrants at one time?"

Rav looked angry. "Yeah, so? So what? They came over here through the official channels, they worked their way up, they assimilated. They didn't land here illegally on a boat and expect to get benefits and a free council house like this lot do. What about all the *British* people who need houses and money to survive?"

"Oh, stop reading *The Daily Mail*," Kate snapped. Then she slammed her empty mug down on the counter and walked away before she said something she would really regret.

She sat back down at her desk, her back to Rav and Olbeck, who she could hear talking together in voices too low for her to understand what they were saying. She stared blankly at her computer screen, a little shaken by the row with Rav, who she'd always got on with so well. Anderton's words to her in his office reoccurred again. *There you go*, she told him silently in her head. *I can be just as hard on my male colleagues, if I feel the need.*

She heard a footstep behind her and turned, to see Olbeck coming up. "You all right?" he asked, pausing by her desk.

"Yes, of course. It's just... I didn't agree with what he was saying."

Olbeck smiled ruefully. "Well, no, nor did I, as a

matter of fact. But, you know, Kate, there's a time and a place..."

"Yes, I know," said Kate, chastened. "Sorry."

"Don't worry about it. I'm sure you and Rav will work it out. He probably feels a bit ashamed of himself now, anyway."

Kate was unconvinced. "Maybe."

"Anyway," said Olbeck. "Let's move on. What next?"

Kate shook herself and sat up a little. "I'd like to interview Ruth Granger again. Clear up this confusion over whether she knew Ali or not. And if she did know him, why pretend that she didn't?"

"Yes, that is odd." Olbeck turned to go and then turned back again. "There was something else I wanted you to look into but I've completely forgotten what it was." He looked into his re-filled mug and sighed. "Maybe it's a three-cup morning. I'll let you know when it comes back to me."

Kate watched him walk back to his office. Then she reached for her mobile, intending to send a text to Chloe to suggest they both go back to the refugee centre in Salterton to talk to Ruth Granger again. She noticed she had a text from Chloe already and read it with a gradually widening smile. Chloe had written *Shall we head back to the refugee centre to interview Ruth Granger? Big discrepancy in her original statement with what the Sanderbys told us. What do you think? Chloe.*

Grinning, Kate texted back, *Great minds. Meet*

you there in half an hour. Then she grabbed her bag and coat and made her way to the door, making a last minute detour around Rav's desk before he could start to tell her about how Islamic State were smuggling jihadis into the country disguised as innocent Syrian refugees.

Chloe and Kate met in the small carpark of the refugee centre.

"By the way," Kate said, as they walked towards the front entrance. "I meant to ask you on our drive back from London but I forgot. What did you think of the Sanderbys?"

Chloe shrugged. "They were much as I expected them to be."

"Which was?"

"Pretentious, phony twats."

Kate snorted a shocked laugh. "Well, maybe a bit, I suppose. They do seem to raise a lot of money for charity, though, don't they?"

Chloe glanced at her. "What I don't get is why they have to raise funds in the first place. That Peregrine is seriously posh, he must have loads of money—look at that house. Why do they need to squeeze it out of everyone else?"

Kate smiled. "Appearances can be deceptive. Half of the aristocracy doesn't have a pot to piss in, apparently."

By now they had reached the entrance hall. It

was stacked with boxes and bags that seemed to have spilled out of the storeroom. A few volunteers were making very little discernible progress in tackling the heap of donations.

Kate asked for Ruth and was directed down a corridor that ran down past the sitting room they had visited on their last visit. At the end of the corridor was a shabby door with a piece of cardboard taped to it that said 'Manager'. Kate stood back, courteously waiting for Chloe to knock.

The room on the other side of the door was tiny, almost a broom cupboard, with just enough room for a small desk, a chair and a filing cabinet. It was lucky that Ruth was so thin, as someone larger would probably not have fitted behind the desk. Kate and Chloe squeezed themselves into the room.

"Sorry, it's bit crowded." Ruth sounded nervous. Her mane of grey hair was twisted up in a topknot, exposing her long thin neck. Kate noticed she seemed to have a bruise at the base of her throat, just above her collarbone. An odd place to have injured yourself, she thought. Then she turned her attention to watching Ruth's face as Chloe held out the photograph of Ali Araya. There was some sort of emotion there, just a flicker on Ruth's face, quickly suppressed.

"Do you know who this man is?"

Ruth looked up. "You asked me this before. I don't know—"

"No, Ms Granger? Are you quite sure you don't know him?"

Now Ruth was looking frightened. A silvery strand of hair slipped downwards from the bundle of hair on top of her head and she brushed it away quickly, tucking it behind her ear. "Well, I wasn't sure... He did look a bit familiar."

"But you couldn't say that you knew him well?" Chloe's tone was hard.

Ruth bit her lip. "I'm not sure."

There was a short silence. Kate was waiting for Ruth to speak, but Chloe obviously decided to go in for the kill.

"This is a man called Ali Araya, Ms Granger. It seems that you did know him, at least well enough to suggest putting his name forward as a speaker at a rally for Sanctuary in July this year."

Ruth's face didn't move but it gradually whitened. For the first time Kate noticed how black her eyebrows were. They stood out like coal smudges against the pale skin of her face. Framed by the silvery halo of her hair, Ruth looked, for a moment, like a ghost.

After a moment she spoke quietly. "I—When I first saw the photograph, I wasn't sure. It did look sort of familiar but I just wasn't sure."

"But if you had an inkling of who he might be, why did you not say?"

Ruth's face flickered. "I don't know. I didn't think it was him."

Chloe brandished the photograph again. "But you recognise him now?"

Ruth's mouth was pulled in at the corners. After a moment, she said tightly "If that's who you say it is, then I'll have to believe you."

Chloe almost hissed in frustration, and Kate wondered whether she should step in. She decided not to. Chloe obviously decided to change tack and spoke again, in a forcedly calm voice. "How well did you know Ali Araya?"

Kate watched Ruth's face keenly and once more saw that almost subliminal flicker.

"Not very well," Ruth said.

"But well enough to know that he would be a good speaker at the Sanctuary rally?"

Ruth looked at Chloe. "Look, do you know how many people I have to deal with every day? Do you know how many refugees come here wanting help? I hear all their stories, the most horrendous stories, and sometimes I have to put them out of my mind or I would just go crazy. So if you're asking why I might have put Ali forward as a speaker, it could have been because he was just the most recent person I'd talked to that day, when I got the request, and his story was fresh in my mind. It doesn't mean I knew him well. After he left, I probably tried to forget what he told me, just as I do a lot of the time." She subsided, chest heaving, angry tears in the corners of her eyes.

Chloe and Kate observed her for a moment, waiting to see if there was anything more but silence fell.

"So, for the record, you say that you didn't know Ali Araya well?" Chloe checked. "Because that will have to go on your statement."

"No, I didn't know him well," Ruth said firmly. She crossed her arms across her chest defensively.

"Right." Chloe looked over at Kate with slightly raised eyebrows. Kate thought she got her meaning.

"Ruth, could you confirm your whereabouts on the night of the second of October please? Specifically between the hours of eleven pm and four am."

Ruth's eyebrows rose. "Me?"

"Yes," said Kate. "You."

For a moment, it looked as though Ruth would protest. Then she closed her opened mouth, swallowed and said, "I was at home, of course. Probably in bed. With my boyfriend."

"Your boyfriend? You live with a partner?"

"Yes," Ruth confirmed but warily. "Why did you want to know?"

"Because he'll need to confirm your account. We'll be contacting him shortly."

Kate saw Ruth's throat ripple as she swallowed again. "Fine."

"Is there anyone else who can confirm your story? Did you see anyone or speak to anyone? Were you on social media?"

Ruth hugged her arms tighter across her body. "I don't think so. I can't remember."

"Well," said Kate. "We'll be speaking to your partner, anyway. What's his name?"

Ruth was staring into space and almost started at Kate's question. "Josh," she said, after a moment. "Josh Beckett."

Kate took down her address details and home telephone number and confirmed that Josh Beckett could currently be found at Ruth's home. Apparently he worked shifts as a hospital porter.

"He might be asleep, though," Ruth said, anxiously. "So, don't—" She broke off.

"It'll be fine, Ms Granger," Kate said. "We won't take up too much of his time."

Chloe put the photograph of Ali Araya back in her briefcase. Kate saw Ruth's gaze flick to it just briefly as the briefcase was closed.

Kate and Chloe went to leave, and at the last moment, Kate turned around. "Is there anything else you'd like to tell us, Ms Granger?" It was a good question to end on—sometimes you got quite surprising revelations as people let their guard down, thinking the questioning had come to an end.

This time, though, it didn't work. Ruth shook her silver head quite firmly. "No," she said. "There's nothing else that I can think of."

Chapter Ten

"Well?" Kate asked her colleague as they walked back to their cars.

Chloe looked grim. "She's definitely keeping something back."

"I think so, too. Worth pulling her in under caution, do you think?"

Chloe had reached her car by now. She fumbled for the keys. "It's certainly something to keep in mind. You know what it's like, though. Everyone's a liar."

Kate opened her own driver's door and slung her hand bag on the passenger seat. "Shall we have a call this afternoon, see where to go from here? I want to get back to the station and see if anything else has come in before we start back on Ruth."

Chloe put her keys in the ignition. "Want me to check on her alibi? As I'm here anyway." She turned the keys and swore as a pitiful grinding sound came from the engine. "Fuck, I don't believe it! It's died again..." Crossly, she yanked at the bonnet lock, jumped out and strode around to the front of the car, pulling up the car bonnet.

Kate and Chloe surveyed the dead car engine with dismay. After a moment, Chloe remarked, "I don't actually know why I'm bothering to look. It's not as if I'm going to be able to fix it."

Kate laughed. The gradually increasing respect for her colleague was beginning to blossom into actual liking. "Come on," she said. "Let's go and check on what's-his-name together and then I can drop you back at the station, if you like."

As they negotiated the narrow streets of Salterton, Kate became aware of Chloe fidgeting a little in the passenger seat next to her. She glanced over. "What's up?"

Chloe looked as though she wasn't going to answer for a second. Then she said, rather abruptly "Look, I've been meaning to say this for a while. I was wrong about you."

"Me?" Kate said in surprise.

"Yes. It's... Well, I've always been able to read people well, get a handle on them and—well, I think I misread you. Or maybe it was something in me that didn't—I didn't mean to—" Chloe sounded increasingly flustered and incoherent. "Perhaps it was me," she finished.

"Well," said Kate, lost for words. "Um. Thanks."

They drove in silence for a moment before Chloe

burst out again. "It's just that you must know what it's like. If you're not a tough bitch to start with you get trodden all over and—I don't know—it just sort of becomes habit. Don't think I don't know what people think of me, half the time. I just can't seem to be able to change."

"There's nothing wrong with how you are," Kate said, rather fiercely. She recalled saying almost the opposite to that to Chloe when she'd slammed the car door and driven off. Now, though, she could sense that Chloe was trying to tell her something important, as well as making Kate an apology of sorts for her previous behaviour. "As a matter of fact, my boss said something similar of me, to be honest."

Chloe looked over at her gratefully. "Yeah?"

"Yes. So we can be tough bitches together." She looked over at Chloe and they exchanged tentative smiles.

It could have been awkward in the car after that, but instead the honest communication seemed to have blown a draft of fresh air between them. Buoyed up, Kate found they had reached Ruth Granger's flat almost before she realised it.

Josh Beckett took a long time to answer the door. When he finally did, he was dressed only in a pair of boxer shorts and a grubby T-shirt and was rubbing sleep from his eyes.

"What do you want?" he muttered, hardly looking at them.

"Police, Mr Beckett." Kate snapped her warrant

card in his face and that woke him up. He looked warily from Kate to Chloe and then back again.

"Yeah?" he asked cautiously.

"May we come in?"

He stood back to let them past. Kate hadn't really given much thought to how she expected to find Ruth's flat, but it was fairly neat and tidy despite obviously having been furnished on a shoe string. There were several framed photographs of Ruth against a variety of exotic locations—Kate recognised the mountains of Macchu Piccu in one, the red rocks of Petra in another—and here and there were dotted interesting little artefacts. Ruth had obviously been a traveller before she settled here in Salterton. Kate looked for evidence of Josh Beckett in the photographs but could see none. Perhaps he had been the one behind the camera.

"We're making enquiries about the death of a man called Ali Araya, Mr Beckett," Kate said. She and Chloe had agreed that she'd do the interview here. "Specifically, we'd like you to confirm whether your partner, Ruth Granger, was here with you on the night of the second October."

Josh Beckett had been slumped on one of the battered armchairs in the room but he gradually straightened up. "Ruth? Here with me on—when was it?"

"The second of October. We're interested in her whereabouts between eleven pm and four am."

Josh rubbed his chin. "Well, I think she was—yeah, she was here with me. For that whole time."

"Can anyone else corroborate your story? Did you or Ruth speak to anyone else that evening? Go on social media?"

Josh was obviously thinking. "Nope. Don't think we saw anyone else. Just watched TV and went to bed."

"We'll need a statement to that effect, Mr Beckett. I can arrange for an officer to come round to take one from you."

Josh looked startled. "What—seriously?"

"Yes. This is a murder investigation, Mr Beckett. If you've got nothing to hide, then you've got nothing to fear."

Josh dropped his gaze to the floor. After a moment, he mumbled "Yeah, I know. It was just a bit of a shock, that's all."

"Is there anything else you'd like to ask us? Or tell us?"

"No." Josh shook his head. "Who was the bloke again?"

Chloe extracted the photograph from her briefcase and handed it to Kate, who handed it to Josh. "Do you know this man?"

Josh was regarding the photograph of the dead man with a frown. "No. I've never seen him before. What was his name?"

"Ali Araya."

Josh continued to regard the picture for another

CELINA GRACE

moment. Then he handed it back. "No," he said more firmly. "Never seen him before in my life."

Back at the car, Kate opened the passenger door for Chloe before unlocking the driver's side. "Think he's telling the truth?"

Chloe shrugged. "Not sure. I suppose Ruth could have phoned him before we got there, got her story straight. Or he might actually be telling the truth and they were at home all evening, on the night of the murder, and have absolutely nothing to do with it."

"What did you think of him?" Kate started up the engine. "Because I got the strange impression that he's kind of a—how shall I put it? He didn't seem to belong in that flat."

"Yeah, I know. Perhaps he's only recently moved in."

Kate was about to drive away when she heard her mobile ringing. Pulling on the handbrake, she scrabbled in her bag to answer it before the caller rang off. It was Rav, which made it a bit awkward.

"Hi, Rav," Kate said, in as normal and 'I'll forget our last words' sort of tone as she could muster. "What's up?"

"Hi, Kate." Rav sounded a little diffident but otherwise normal. "Are you heading back here soon? Because Salterton have sent over some CCTV footage that could be interesting."

"Really?" Kate found herself glancing over at Chloe

involuntarily, who met her gaze with eyebrows raised. "I've just finished up an interview so I'll be back soon."

She said goodbye and ended the call.

"Something come up?" asked Chloe.

"Yes—your lot have sent over some CCTV footage that might be important. Do you know anything about it?"

Chloe shook her head. "Nope. I've been with you all morning, haven't I?"

Kate put the car into gear and began to drive off. "Do you want me to drop you off at Salterton?" A thought struck her. "Or why not just come back to Abbeyford with me and we can view it together?"

"Okay." Chloe sounded pleased to be asked.

The traffic was light and it only took them twenty minutes to drive back to Abbeyford from Salterton. Kate ushered Chloe into the office, realising seconds later, with a qualm, that she'd spent quite a lot of time slagging this woman off to her companions. They weren't to know of her change of mind.

Praying that nobody would say anything embarrassing, Kate introduced Chloe to Theo and to Rav. Olbeck was closeted in his office, with the door shut, so that was one introduction that could be put off for the moment. It was interesting to observe Chloe's reaction to her colleagues. Rav, who had thankfully stopped channelling the UKIP manifesto, was normally polite and friendly, and Chloe was perfectly normal and friendly back to him. Theo, however, made it a bit too obvious that he found Chloe attractive and Kate could almost see the old Chloe—brusque and prickly—descending upon her like a costume. Theo, luckily, was a bit too thick-skinned to realise he was being snubbed and offered to go and make drinks. Kate sent up a fervent prayer that he wouldn't ask Chloe if she liked her coffee like she liked her men.

"So what is it that you've got to show us?" she asked Rav.

He gestured for them to follow him to his desk. Once there, he brought up the video footage file that Salterton Station had already sent over.

"This is from High Street, about nine o'clock on the night of the murder. Well, look for yourself," he added, gesturing to the rapidly changing time clock in one corner of the screen. "Here's our victim, coming out of this street there and walking down until we lose him as he goes off camera."

The women watched the footage. Ali Araya, clad in a bulky duffle coat and blue jeans, with white trainers on his feet, walked quite slowly down the pavement of Salterton High Street, looking in shop windows from time to time, his hands in his pockets. He looked calm, relaxed, unhurried, clearly never thinking that somewhere there, up in the future, lay his assailant and his death on the sandy shores of Muddiford Beach.

"Clothes!" cried a voice behind them and both Kate and Chloe jumped. Kate turned around to see Olbeck standing behind them with both hands raised in the air, palms turned outward.

"Sorry?" asked Chloe.

Olbeck seemed to realise who she was. "Oh, hello DS Wapping, I didn't know you were here." Kate caught the quick quizzical glance he gave her. "Yes, clothes. That was what I wanted to talk to you about, Kate. I'd forgotten until now." He moved between the two women, grabbed the mouse to pause the footage that was now replaying. Ali Araya froze in his slow stroll down the street. "Look. Look at what he's wearing. That's the night of the murder, right? When we found the body, what was he wearing?"

For a moment, Rav, Kate and Chloe looked at him blankly. Then Rav gasped and began to rummage for a file on his crowded desk top. He flicked through the various bits of paper within it and extracted one, reading aloud from it.

"Faded black jeans, a black T-shirt. No underwear, no shoes, no socks."

"Exactly," said Olbeck, with a satisfied smile. "Now, given that in this footage he's currently wearing a thick coat, blue jeans, trainers and socks, why the hell did his body end up wearing such different clothes?"

"That's right," Kate said slowly, thinking about the implications. "Either he changed clothes—why, though? Why go for a walk on a cold night on a beach in the few clothes he was wearing?"

"I suppose he wouldn't go for a night swim or something," Chloe murmured. Then she shook her head impatiently. "No, of course not. Especially since he'd almost drowned coming over from Eritrea."

"It's not very probable," Olbeck agreed. "The most likely explanation is that the murderer dressed him in the clothes we found him in. Why, though?"

They were all silent for a moment, looking at the frozen image of the dead man on screen. Kate wondered if the others were thinking what she was—how strange it was to see a man looking so calm and unworried when you knew what was awaiting him that night. To Kate, he was so clearly marked for death it was as if a black-robed skeleton stood behind him, bony fingers reaching for him, just out of sight.

Chapter Eleven

"LISTEN," SAID CHLOE. "YOU DON'T have to keep running me here and there all over the place. I can easily get a taxi."

"It's fine." Kate was already reaching for her bag and car keys. "What *is* the matter with your car, anyway?"

"It's ten years old and knackered."

"Clearly. A new battery would probably be a good start."

"A new car would be even better," Chloe said, grinning. She looked about a hundred times prettier smiling, Kate thought.

"Seriously though, I'm happy to drop you home. I—" Kate hesitated for a moment. "I feel like dropping back in at the refugee centre. Just to see how things are there."

Chloe yawned. "I think I'll leave you to it, this time. I'm about as done-in as my car."

The drive to Chloe's house took about half an hour. She lived on the seaward side of Salterton, in a tiny fisherman's cottage, half a mile from the centre of town. The cottage's front door opened directly onto the street and it looked as though it were constructed of sugar cubes. Kate expressed her open and honest admiration.

"I love it," Chloe admitted, ushering Kate through the front door. "I bought it about three years ago, when I split up with my husband. It's the first place I've ever lived where it's been truly *mine*."

"I didn't know you'd been married." Kate stood in the small living room, noting the old but well-made furniture, the vase of bright orange dahlias on the mantelpiece, the pretty ornaments and bright cushions.

"I wasn't for long. He got a transfer soon after we split up. Just as well—could have been very awkward working together after that."

"He was an officer?" Kate wasn't surprised. Out of most of her colleagues, the ones who seemed to have successful marriages were married to other police officers. At least then you knew what you were getting into. Tin came into her mind, just as Chloe asked her a question.

"Are you married, Kate?"

"No. I have a boyfriend, though, Tin. He's a journalist."

"Oh, right," Chloe said, sounding surprised. "What sort of stuff does he write?"

Kate elaborated. Chloe listened and then exclaimed.

"Oh! I know him. Good looking black guy, he's writing about the migrant crisis at the moment, isn't he? I've been reading his stuff in *The Guardian*."

Kate concurred that Tin was indeed that journalist. She felt quite proud to be associated with him, given Chloe's obvious admiration. At the same time, she felt a stab of guilt that, given her current workload, she'd hardly been very supportive or encouraging of his career lately. *We must meet up soon; we'll have forgotten what each other looks like.*

Chloe urged Kate to stay for a cup of tea but Kate, honestly pleased that they seemed to be getting on so well, declined regretfully. "I must get to the centre before it closes."

"Why are you going again? Thinking of having another go at Ruth?"

"I don't know," said Kate, unable to articulate exactly why she wanted to go back. Intuitively, it was just something she felt she should do.

Chloe saw her to the door, yawning again. "Good luck," she said.

"I'll update you first thing tomorrow," Kate promised, saying goodbye.

Driving to the centre, Kate found herself thinking about Chloe and her precious little cottage. Being inside it had instantly recalled her own house; the way it was clean and tidy and lovingly decorated and furnished. A house cherished by its owner, just as

109

Kate cherished her own home. It was another sharp reminder that she and Chloe had a lot in common. Hadn't Anderton said something like that? She felt annoyed at him for being so perspicacious. Was she, Kate, really that obvious? *Perhaps he's just studied you very closely* whispered a naughty little voice and she grimaced and turned the radio on to try and drown out the thoughts in her head.

She drove to the centre, parked the car in the nearly empty car park, next to a black BMW which, judging by the number plate, was the very newest model. Its luxurious appearance contrasted oddly with the scruffy surroundings. The sun was setting but its rosy glow was dimming, blotted out by gathering grey clouds. For the first time, Kate could sense the promise of winter in the chill twilight air, and she hurried towards the entrance, wishing she had worn something a little warmer.

Kate closed the glass door of the entrance hall behind her. She could hear the sounds of clothing being packed and unpacked in the main hall—obviously a couple of dedicated volunteers were still there, still wading through the pile of donations. Kate hesitated, wondering whether she should introduce herself and see if they could help. She'd decided that she was here to try and see if the clothes Ali Araya had been wearing when his body was found would be recognised, by Ruth or by the volunteers. She was still uncertain as to whether they could legitimately pull Ruth in for interviewing under caution, but she decided she would run the suggestion past Anderton in the morning and get his approval before she and Chloe did so.

Better talk to Ruth first—she was the manager, after all. Kate looked for her in the little sitting room, which was empty. Then she made her way down the corridor and knocked at Ruth's office door. Nobody answered.

Perhaps she'd already left for the day. Kate stood indecisively for a moment, shifting from foot to foot. Perhaps—but her train of thought was interrupted when she realised she could hear somebody crying.

Where was the sound coming from? Kate looked around, trying to work out the source of the sobs. After a moment, she spotted a door which obviously led to the ladies' toilets. Without hesitating, she pushed it open.

It was a small space, just enough room for a sink and two cubicles. There were two people already there. One was Ruth, who had her hands to her face and was sobbing. The other, to Kate's considerable surprise, was Nuria Sanderby. All three women exclaimed as they caught sight of one another.

Kate was the first to recover. "Sorry to push in. I was hoping to have a quick chat with Ruth."

"Poor Ruth's rather upset at the moment," Nuria said, rather unnecessarily given the tears that were flowing freely down Ruth's thin cheeks.

"Oh dear," said Kate. She looked at Ruth with her eyebrows slightly raised.

Ruth scrubbed at her eyes. Her hair was loose now, falling in a silvery cloud around her shoulders. "I'm all right," she muttered, after a moment. Nuria, who had a protective arm around her shoulders, handed her a tissue. "Thanks."

Kate continued to look at Ruth. The intention in her gaze must have stung because, after a moment, Ruth said defensively, "I'm not upset because of anything to do with Ali—I mean, to do with the case. It's a personal matter."

Kate nodded. She wondered whether Ruth had confided in Nuria and, if so, whether Nuria would be forthcoming with the information.

There was a slightly awkward moment of silence and then Nuria asked, "What can we do for you, DS Redman?"

"Call me Kate, please." Kate needed this woman on her side. "I just had a quick question for Ruth, if she has a moment."

Ruth was looking down at the dirty tiled floor, her eyes red. "Does it have to be now?"

"It won't take long. I just wanted to ask you if you could identify the clothes Ali Araya was wearing when his—" Kate hesitated, given Ruth's current emotional state. "Um, the clothes he was wearing when his body was found?"

She braced herself but Ruth seemed puzzled more than upset. "I'm sorry?" she asked, frowning.

This would have been easier without Nuria standing there, like a mother hen, Kate thought. She wondered whether it was worth the hassle of asking her to leave and decided it probably wasn't.

She explained to both women that the CCTV footage of Ali's clothing before his death and the clothes he was wearing afterwards didn't match.

"How extraordinary," said Nuria. She moved away from Ruth a little. "Why on Earth would that have happened?" A moth flew in at the open window, clearly attracted by the strip light, and she batted at it absently as it flew past her face.

"That's what we're hoping to find out," Kate said. She described the clothes on the body. "Black T-shirt, a faded black pair of jeans. There were no labels but the quality was quite poor. Does that sound familiar to either of you?"

She knew as soon as she asked it that it was a pointless question. Nuria was shaking her head with a look of faint distaste. Looking at her own white get-up, Kate would be prepared to bet that she wore nothing less than designer labels at all times. Ruth still looked puzzled. "I never saw Ali wearing anything like that before. He used to wear charity shop clothes, of course he did, they're cheap and he had no money. But they were always quite good quality."

That was a striking observation from someone

who claimed that she hadn't known the victim well. Kate felt a renewed urge to get the OK from Anderton to interview Ruth further.

"Well, thank you for your time, ladies," she said, preparing to go. "Ms Granger, we may need to talk to you again."

Ruth looked scared, and as if sensing that, Nuria put her arm back around her. They said nothing as Kate said goodbye, but as she closed the toilet door behind her, she could hear the murmur of their voices start up again.

Resisting the urge to put her ear to the door, Kate made her way to the exit. She asked the two remaining volunteers if they could identify the clothing she described and drew a blank both times. *Bit of a wasted journey, Kate.* She gave a philosophical shrug and left.

She was walking around the back of the building to where she'd parked her car when a dark shadow detached itself from the building and came towards her. She started and then relaxed once she'd seen who was approaching her. Although she'd only ever seen the woman once, she recognised her immediately as the woman she'd seen on her first visit to the centre, who'd averted her eyes from Kate in what had looked like fear.

Now, though, the woman seemed less afraid. Even so, there was the sense that she was bracing herself for the contact. Kate stopped walking and let the woman come to her.

"Are you a police woman?" asked the woman. She had a strong accent but her English was perfect.

"Yes, that's right. I'm Detective Sergeant Kate Redman. Can I help you?"

The woman hesitated. She wasn't pretty—her nose was a little too long, her jaw too wide for beauty—but she had beautiful dark eyes. There was character in her face, something of strength that suggested the owner had suffered but survived. "You are investigating the death of Ali Araya, is that correct?"

"Yes," Kate said, alert now. "Do you have any information on that case?"

The woman didn't speak for a moment. Then she said slowly, "It may be nothing. But perhaps not. I will tell you."

Kate waited. The woman put a hand up to touch her headscarf, perhaps to adjust it, perhaps even for some sort of comfort. "I am Nada. Ali and I were friends. We didn't know each other very long, and I am sure we didn't know each other very well, but we spent some time together. He was a very charming person, he liked to laugh. He cheered me up."

"Your English is amazing," Kate commented, unable to help herself.

Nada smiled. "Thank you. I was educated in England but I returned to Syria for my university education." Her face darkened. "I became a teacher at one of the women's colleges when I graduated. But I had to leave."

115

Kate waited. After a moment, Nada swallowed and said "I was forced to leave Syria very quickly, my life was in danger. My sister helped me, because she knew that if I stayed I would be killed. Wafaa, my partner... My partner was taken and tortured by the police. She died."

Kate put a hand up to her mouth. "I'm—I'm so sorry. That's awful." Once again, just as in the Sanctuary head office, she was aware of the inadequacy of her words.

Nada looked away. Kate could see tears in her eyes. "To be gay in Syria now is to walk with a death sentence. If the police do not catch you, then ISIS does. Whichever way, you are dead. It is only a question of how much you suffer before they kill you." She turned her gaze back to Kate. "Poor Wafaa was raped many times before she died. I know this. That is what would have happened to me. It is a death sentence."

For some reason, Kate found herself thinking of that frozen image of Ali Araya on the night of his death and her fanciful imagining of Death stood behind him, just out of sight. She found it difficult to repress a shiver.

Nada spoke again. "My sister managed to get some papers and I took a flight out that very next night, when we knew what had happened to Wafaa. My sister took a very great risk. I am sick with worry for her, back in Syria. I don't know what might have happened." For a moment, she closed her eyes. "Sometimes I don't think I can actually live with the fear, it is so great."

Kate put an impulsive hand on Nada's arm. "I'm so sorry to hear all the terrible things you've gone through."

Nada smiled painfully. "Ali was very sympathetic too. He knew what it was like to live in such a place."

"Was Ali gay too?" asked Kate curiously.

Nada actually laughed. "Not at all! Ali loved women. Too much, I think. He was what you might call—what is the saying? A 'ladies' man'."

"I see," said Kate. "What was it that you wanted to tell me?"

Nada became serious again. "It was just something that he said to me once. I was talking about the shelter, and the good that it does, and he said something like 'She's not who you think she is, you know.'"

"Who was 'she'?" asked Kate.

"Ruth. The lady that runs the shelter."

Kate frowned. "Did he say why? Did he say any more?"

Nada shook her head. "I was about to ask him what he meant but he put his hand up to his mouth and said, 'Forget it, forget I said that. I didn't mean it.' And he didn't say any more."

Kate was silent for a moment, thinking. Nada added, "I think he and Ruth may have—may have had a relationship. I don't know for sure, but it was just the way—the way they were together. I had a feeling that they had become, or they had been, involved with one another."

"Sexually, you mean?"

Nada looked a little embarrassed. "I think so. But, of course, I don't know for certain. Ali didn't say anything to me."

A cold wind had sprung up, bringing the briny scent of the sea towards them. Kate shivered now and saw Nada do the same.

"Thank you, Nada, for telling me. May I give you my card? If there's anything else you think might be important, please don't hesitate to call me."

She handed over her card into Nada's cold hand. Kate's teeth were almost chattering.

"I must go," said Nada, obviously equally chilly. "I hope I have been of some assistance."

"You have. Please do contact me if you think of anything else, even if you think it might not be important."

"I will." Nada drew her coat tighter about her and turned to go. Then she turned back. "I miss Ali. I want to help you catch who killed him."

"Thank you," Kate said, steadily. She watched Nada walk away across the deserted car park. Then she scurried for her car, shivering with cold.

She was running the heater full blast, waiting for the car to warm up before she drove away, when she saw Nuria Sanderby coming towards her from the centre. Of course, the BMW must be Nuria's car... Kate wondered whether she should drive off but Nuria had a purposeful look on her face and was heading straight for Kate. Kate reluctantly wound down her driver-side window, hoping that Nuria wasn't going to give her a bollocking for upsetting her staff.

"I'm sorry to bother you, DS Redman. I won't keep you, I just wanted to try and explain what was upsetting Ruth."

Relieved she wasn't going to be shouted at, Kate nodded encouragingly. Nuria hugged her cashmere coat tighter towards her and leant forward a little. She was wearing a perfume that Kate couldn't place but it smelt rich and exotic. Just like Nuria, she thought with an inner grin.

"Ruth's been having some relationship issues for a while. She wouldn't tell me anything more tonight, about why exactly she was upset, but she mentioned Josh's name a couple of times." Nuria's delicate dark brows drew together in a frown. "I can't say I think much of him but—well, it's not my place to judge."

"That's why she was crying?" Kate could feel the heater in her car finally starting to pump out some warm air which, currently, was going straight back out of the open window.

"Yes. I dropped in for a quick visit, while I was in the area, and found her in a terrible state. I've been trying to calm her down ever since I got here." She looked at the gold watch on her slender wrist. "And now I'm late for a fundraising dinner back in London."

"Why were you in the area?" asked Kate. "It's a fair way from London, isn't it?"

Nuria looked at her in surprise. "Oh, but we have a second home here. Didn't you know? Just along the coast. It's such a gorgeous part of the world. I thought I'd come down for a few days before the weather gets really cold."

How the other half live, thought Kate. One house is clearly not enough.

"Well, I'll say goodbye," said Nuria, straightening up. "I must fly, I'm going to be hideously late."

"Just one minute," said Kate. "What would you say to the idea that Ruth Granger and Ali Araya were in a sexual relationship?"

Nuria looked shocked. "What? Oh, that can't be right. That can't be true." Anger vibrated in her voice. "That would be very inappropriate, for one thing. Oh, that *can't* be true." Her cheeks had reddened with the cold, or with emotion. "Who told you that?"

"I can't say at the moment," Kate said. "I'm not sure that it's true anyway."

Nuria looked a little relieved. "I'm quite sure it's not."

"Well," said Kate, longing to get her window up and get warm. "Thanks for letting me know about Ruth."

"That's quite all right. I'll be sure to be in touch if I hear anything else. And now I really *must* dash. Goodbye."

Kate didn't wait to see her get into the Beamer. Instead she thankfully rolled up the window and drove to the exit. Perhaps the visit hadn't been such a waste of time after all.

Chapter Twelve

KATE WOKE THE NEXT MORNING to golden sunlight pouring in through the gap in her bedroom curtains. She lay warm and cosy in her bed and, without thinking, reached across for Tin. The other side of the bed was empty and she immediately remembered that he was up in London for the week, meeting with his editor and filing his most recent story. Kate felt vaguely disappointed. Then again, it was nice to have the bed to herself... She stretched luxuriously, got up and pottered off to the bathroom.

Her mobile phone was never far from her side, and as she soaped herself down under the gush of hot water, she heard it clattering on the top of the bathroom cabinet as it rang. Groping her way out of the shower, she picked it up gingerly with wet hands, seeing Anderton's name flash at her from the screen.

"Morning, sir."

"Morning. Sorry to wake you with bad news but we've found a body. Apparent suicide."

"Oh dear." Kate felt surprisingly naked, talking to

Anderton like this. Well, she *was* naked but she felt as if he might be able to see her, even over the phone line. She grabbed a towel and wrapped it around herself, tucking the phone between her chin and her shoulder.

Anderton's tone was grim. "There's more. Guess where we found it?"

Kate was at a loss. "Um—"

"Sorry, I shouldn't play games this early in the morning. I'm at Muddiford Beach."

There was a draft coming from somewhere and Kate shivered as the cool air hit her wet skin. "What? Another body on the beach?"

"It seems they threw themselves off the cliffs. Bit of a mess, to be honest."

"Oh, God." Kate closed her eyes momentarily. "Okay, let me get dressed and I'll be right there." A thought struck here. "Is it a man or a woman?"

"Woman. She left her handbag at the top of the cliffs, so that was a piece of luck. She's already been identified. Her name was Nada Qabbani."

Kate straightened up in shock and the towel slipped to the floor. "*Nada*? Oh my *god*. If it's her—I think I spoke to her just last night. She had some information about Ali Araya."

"*What*?" Anderton's voice cut like steel down the line.

"I know. She told me—well, look I'll tell you when I get there. I'll be as quick as I can."

She said goodbye and hurried to turn the shower

off. She gave herself a cursory rub down and flung on some clothes. Then she quickly fed Merlin, who was meowing loudly downstairs in the kitchen, grabbed her coat and keys and ran out to the car.

Driving to Muddiford Beach, Kate could feel herself clenching her teeth. Was it the woman who had spoken to her last night? It seemed likely. Had Nada killed herself? Kate went over their conversation in her mind, trying to remember exactly what Nada had told her. She had been suffering, that was clear—grieving for her dead lover, anxious for her sister. What was it she had said? Kate thought back, remembered Nada's dark eyes fixed upon hers as she spoke. *Sometimes I don't think I can actually live with the fear, it is so great.* Had that been it? Had Nada's fear, and the great pain of her loss, overwhelmed her at last?

Kate saw the brown road sign for Muddiford Beach up ahead and flicked on her indicator. If it was Nada... If Nada had indeed killed herself, was it because her conversation with Kate had brought all of her fear and worry to the forefront of her mind? Did that mean, if that were the case, that Kate herself bore some responsibility for her death? *Of course not,* Kate told herself scathingly, but there was still a little ache of guilt somewhere inside her. She knew why that was. It was because, no matter how much you tried to help, there was always a feeling that you could have done more. That you *should* have done more, even if you didn't realise there was more to be done. It was horrible, that feeling; corrosive and bitter. Kate set her jaw as she parked the car, swallowing down her anger and shame.

As she walked towards the top of the steps, she could see the blue and white flutter of police tape, oddly jaunty in this sunshine and this location. She was struck with déjà vu—coming here when Ali Araya's body was found, wondering what condition it would be in. If Nada had hurled herself from the clifftops, a hundred feet from the beach itself, then the result would quite probably be terrible. Kate braced herself as she reached the final step and walked towards the small group of people she could see at the foot of the rock face.

She took one look at the body as she got closer, enough to see that it was the woman she'd spoken to last night, and then resolutely turned her eyes away. It was as bad as she'd been imagining. What was left of what had been poor Nada was lying some fifteen feet from the officers but the sand and pebbles around the body were splashed and stained with blood and other unidentifiable body matter in a grim circumference. Kate swallowed down the nausea as best she could, thanking God that she hadn't yet eaten breakfast.

Anderton turned as she got closer. "Good morning." He looked closer and, obviously noting her pallor, added in concern, "You okay?"

"I'll be fine." Kate was deliberately not looking at the body but it seemed to pull at the corners of her vision like some awful Halloween sideshow. "It's not a very nice sight, is it?"

"No," agreed Anderton. "Poor woman."

Olbeck and Theo were also there. Olbeck gave Kate a quick, friendly squeeze and she gave him a grateful smile.

"So," Anderton said. "As I mentioned, before Kate got here, she met the victim last night. It *is* her, I presume?"

"Yes," said Kate. "She's still wearing the same clothes as she was yesterday."

"Can you tell us what you two talked about, Kate?"

Kate nodded. She explained the gist of the conversation she'd had with Nada and the idea that Nada had shared that Ruth Granger and Ali Araya may have been sexually involved. "Now, she did say she wasn't certain," Kate explained. "She said she just thought it was likely, from the way they acted around one another."

"Did she say anything else?"

Kate thought. "Yes, there was one thing that struck me. She said that Ali had told her that Ruth—well, he'd said something like 'she's not who you think she is'. But he didn't say anything else."

"What was it exactly that Ali said to Nada? Can you remember?"

Kate screwed up her face in concentration. "She

said *he* said 'she's not who you think she is'. That was it, I think. Nada said Ali clammed up then and didn't—or wouldn't—say any more."

"Hmm." Anderton rubbed his chin, unshaven that morning and grey with stubble. "Now, people, let's marshal our thoughts. One of the most likely explanations for this death is suicide, yes? This is a well-known suicide spot, for one. Why the council don't put some bloody great fences up at the top is a mystery, but there you go."

"They keep promising they're going to do that," Olbeck chipped in. "But then they never do. Probably not cost-effective, or something."

"Huh. They have enough money to bully us into doing more recycling, I notice. But I digress. Oh, here comes Atwell's lot, now."

As one, they all looked up and saw the Salterton team approaching. Kate saw Chloe's blonde head amongst them and was happy to find that she was actually pleased to see her.

Atwell was the first to reach them, his round face dewed with perspiration. "By Christ, you're quick off the mark, Anderton." He made a moue of disgust as he glanced at the body. "God, what a mess. I hear she's been identified?" Anderton nodded. "Just as well," Atwell added with a grimace.

Chloe came over to where Kate and Olbeck were standing, and they exchanged quick smiles, suitably toned down to fit the sombre occasion.

"SOCO are here now," Chloe said. "They followed us into the car park."

Kate could see the white-clad figures descending the cliff steps. She felt a sudden jump of paranoia that she would see Tin amongst them, come to report on the incident, before reminding herself that he was in London.

"Press can't be far behind," she remarked.

"No," said Anderton. "We'd better—"

Atwell interrupted him. "I've already got several of my uniforms up there," he said with an admonitory frown. "So you don't need to worry about that."

"Champion," Anderton said heartily. "Would you give me and my team a few moments, George?"

As the Abbeyford team congregated into a huddle, Chloe looked as though she wasn't sure whether to stay or go. Just as Kate was opening her mouth to ask her to stay, Chloe gave a sort of half-shrug and walked back to where her Salterton teammates were standing.

"Right," said Anderton. He hadn't seemed to notice Chloe leaving. "Now, where were we?"

"You were saying it's most probably a suicide," Olbeck said.

"Yes, exactly. Here we have a very traumatised, very stressed young woman, who's been through some horrible things. She'd lost her partner, and her family, and her country, and then she's lost her friend, right here on this beach. It's not a great stretch to imagine that everything just overwhelmed her and she decided to end it."

"I don't suppose she left a note?" asked Kate.

Anderton shook his head. "Not here. There's nothing like that in her bag. We haven't had a look at where she lived, yet, though. She may have left something there." He cleared his throat. "So, that's possibility one. Any other ideas?"

"I've been thinking," Theo said in a low voice. They all looked at him expectantly. "You know that case, you know, with the young girls from that Catholic mission place? The butterfly killer. Remember how we kept finding bodies in the same place? Well, what if it's the same sort of thing?"

The same thought had actually occurred to Kate. She was glad she hadn't voiced it when she heard Anderton snort. "No, Theo. Not possible."

"It might be—"Theo began defensively, but Anderton cut him off.

"No. There is no way that this is the work of another serial killer. Different victims, different MO, there's just no similarity."

"But—"Theo protested but Anderton wasn't finished yet.

"Name me one serial killer who kills across genders. Go on, name me one."

They all thought furiously for a moment before they all looked at one another and shrugged.

"All right," said Theo. "But what if it's something

like that? Some racist vigilantes targeting asylum seekers or something like that?"

"Well," Anderton conceded. "It's a possibility." Kate wondered if she were the only one to hear the unspoken sentence that followed his words. *A bloody unlikely one, but there you go.* "Anyone else got any ideas?"

Kate spoke up. What she said had been the thought that had dogged her all the way from her home. "What if somebody was worried that Nada knew something, perhaps something in connection with Ali Araya's death, and they killed her?"

They were all silent for a moment. Anderton looked at her steadily. "Yes. Yes, I'm afraid I've thought that was a possibility too."

Kate went on. "I don't know if she had anything else to tell me. If she did, I wonder why she didn't tell me last night?"

"Oh, that's easy." Olbeck took another look at the grim remains of what had once been a living, breathing, loving person. He said, sadly, "She had to know whether she could trust you or not."

"Yes." Kate thought about that and nodded. "I did get the impression that she was—well, testing the waters."

"So if she did know something, then someone had to silence her." Anderton voiced what they were all thinking.

"How can we possibly tell?" Olbeck asked.

"Well, we've still got the PM," said Anderton. "But unless the pathologist finds a bloody great handprint in the middle of her back, it's probably not going to get us much further. But you never know."

As Anderton was speaking, Kate could see the little huddle of Salterton detectives break up. She saw Atwell and Chloe detach themselves and begin to walk over towards them. Anderton clearly saw them too. "Right," he said hurriedly. "Let's confer back at base. Someone needs to stay here, see if preliminary forensics dig up anything important."

"I'll do it," Theo said, just as Atwell and Chloe joined them.

"Looks like a bit more cooperation is called for, eh?" said Atwell. He took out a tissue and mopped his glistening forehead. "Shall we take a trip back to Salterton and have a chat about things?"

"Of course," Anderton said. "All right, team. We'll touch base later. Theo, give me a call if anything comes up."

As the two meetings broke up, and the Scene of Crime officers began to erect a white tent around the body, Chloe and Kate walked back to their cars. A helicopter buzzed overhead, and Chloe glanced up at it with a scowl. "That's got to be press."

"Yes," sighed Kate. She gave thanks once again that Tin was far away in London. "Has anything come up from your side that we should know about?"

"Not so far. I guess you guys are thinking what we're thinking?"

"Which is?"

"That this death could be linked to the death of Ali Araya?"

Kate stopped climbing for a second, puffed out. "Yes, that's the gist. Although, as Anderton has pointed out, it could just as easily have been a suicide. Did you know I talked to her last night, the victim, I mean?"

"No," Chloe said, clearly startled. "What happened?"

Kate filled her in, finishing up just as they reached the car park.

"God, the poor woman," Chloe said, grimacing. "It seems hard to believe things like that are happening here and now, doesn't it?" She lowered her voice. "Have you seen that awful video doing the rounds, you know, where ISIS throw the gay guy off a roof?"

"No," Kate said in horror. "I would never watch something like that."

"Me neither," Chloe said hurriedly. "But they were talking about it at the station. It's horrible. He survives the fall but then they stone him to d—"

"Please." Kate held up a hand, feeling as if she'd had enough gore and violence for one day.

"Sorry. It's just it got me thinking." Chloe was fumbling for her keys, her cheeks rather red. "What with Nada being gay and, you know, being found at the bottom of a cliff."

Kate stared at her. "What are you suggesting?"

"Nothing, I'm just thinking, that's all."

"You're not seriously suggesting that we might have some ISIS members around here who are defenestrating gay people?"

Chloe straightened up, properly flushed now. "I said I didn't have any theories. It just reminded me of that bloody video, okay?" Her tone was rapidly climbing towards anger.

Kate felt the same annoyance begin to seep through her. "Well, that's a really stupid idea," she snapped, forgetting that Theo had advanced a theory equally as far-fetched.

"Well, fucking forget it then," Chloe spat back in much the same tone of voice. Then she turned and marched away towards her car.

Steaming with anger, Kate stood still for a moment. She looked back at the top of the cliffs and at the huge, glittering, indifferent body of water beyond it. Even here, she could hear the endless waves breaking upon the shore. Nada—had she jumped or was she pushed? The end result was the same; she was dead, smashed to pieces.

Kate took a deep breath and ran after Chloe, who was just getting into her car. "Wait. Wait, Chloe."

For a moment she thought Chloe was going to drive off over her foot. Then the other woman yanked on the handbrake with ill grace and wound down the driver-side window.

"Look, I'm sorry," Kate panted. "I'm sorry not to have listened. It's as good a theory as any."

For a moment Chloe stared at her, frowning. Then she smiled reluctantly. "No, it's not, it's ridiculous. You and I both know that if anything, Nada was killed because she knew something about Ali Araya's death."

Kate stared at her. "Yes. Exactly."

"Who else was at the centre when you were talking to Nada?"

Kate thought. "Ruth Granger and Nuria Sanderby. Two volunteers, I didn't get their names. There may have been other people there, but I didn't see them."

Chloe tapped her steering wheel. "And Ali said something about Ruth wasn't to be trusted?"

"Well—something like that."

"Hmm." Chloe looked lost in thought for a moment. "I guess we could at least ascertain whether Nuria Sanderby did go up to London, as she said she did."

"Yes, that's a good start."

Chloe nodded, a quick sharp bob of her head. "That should be easy enough to check. CCTV and a call to whoever was holding this fundraising dinner. Leave that with me."

"Thanks." Kate straightened up. She could see Anderton and Atwell walking across the car park. "If I'm not very much mistaken, the first thing *we'll* be doing is pulling in Ruth Granger for an interview."

"Well, good luck with that. I'll let you know if I find anything on Nuria."

"Thanks," Kate said again. She smiled her goodbye and stepped back, allowing Chloe to drive away. Then she walked over to where Anderton and Atwell were standing, talking. She reached them just as they shook hands and parted.

"Oh, Kate," Anderton said. "Good. We need to go and get Ruth Granger down to the station."

Bingo, thought Kate, hiding a smile. Out loud she said "Of course, sir. Mark and I will go and bring her in."

"Good stuff. See you back at the station then."

"Goodbye," said Kate. She walked back to her car, realising the interior would be like an oven after sitting in the sun for several hours. She opened both front doors to try and get some air through the vehicle. As she waited for the car to cool down, she watched the seagulls wheeling through the air above her and thought about Nada.

In a moment of sentimentality, she imagined Nada and Wafaa reunited in the afterlife, together once more. *I hope that's true*, she told the spectral image of the dark-eyed woman she held in her mind's eye. *I hope you find one other again*. Then, sniffing a little, she got back in the now cooler car and drove away.

Chapter Thirteen

UNDER THE HARSH STRIP LIGHTS of the interview room, Ruth Granger looked thinner and paler than ever. Her silver hair looked white under the glare from the ceiling. As she nervously sat down, her loose sleeve fell away from her slender wrist and Kate caught a glimpse of what looked like a round, red sore. She only saw it for a second before Ruth pulled the sleeve back down over her wrist.

Anderton and Kate sat down opposite her. Anderton had just spoken the date and the time of the interview, and was opening his mouth to begin the questions, when there was a knock on the door. All three of them, plus the duty solicitor who sat beside Ruth, looked over enquiringly at Theo, who had poked his head around the door.

"Sorry to interrupt, but Kate, Chloe's on the phone."

Kate excused herself and ran upstairs to the office, where the telephone receiver on her desk was lying on its side. "Hello?"

"Hi, it's Chloe. I just thought I'd let you know that

I've looked into Nuria Sanderby's movements last night. There's clear footage of her car heading towards the M4, although we haven't really got anything before that, in Salterton itself, apart from when she left the carpark at the centre. She's also spotted at various points on the motorway itself, heading towards London. So that tallies with what she told us."

"Right," said Kate, scribbling notes.

"I also called the Sanctuary office and got the number for the people who were organising the fundraiser she said she was attending. God, that secretary's a cold fish, isn't she?"

Thinking of her first impressions of Chloe herself, Kate couldn't help a grin. Out loud, she agreed.

"Anyway," Chloe continued. "I spoke to the organisers. Nuria turned up late but she seemed quite normal. A bit quiet and serious, but I guess that's not suspicious in itself."

"What about her husband?" Kate asked. "Was he there?"

"Yes, he got there before Nuria, apparently."

"Okay," said Kate. "So that clears both of them, really, doesn't it?"

"Pretty much."

Kate sighed; whether in relief or in annoyance she wasn't sure. "Okay, well, thanks for checking, Chloe."

"No worries. How are you getting on with Ruth?"

"We've just started. I'd better get back there, actually."

"Okay. Let's talk later."

The two women said their farewells and then Kate pelted back down the stairs, anxious that she'd missed something important. It had been quite a while since she and Anderton had interviewed a suspect together, and it was a little disconcerting to find how much she'd missed the way they worked together.

Ruth Granger wasn't yet crying but it looked as though tears were not far away. She sat upright, her lips compressed, little lines of tension cut into her forehead.

"So, you did know Ali Araya somewhat better than you first indicated to DS Redman, here?" Anderton was saying as Kate re-entered the room.

Ruth's gaze flicked to Kate and then back down to her hands, clasped in her lap. "Well, I—I got a bit confused..."

Anderton waited. Then, when she trailed off into silence, he pushed for more clarity. "You weren't sure that it was the same man in the photograph as the one you knew?"

Ruth nodded uncertainly. Kate wondered whether Ruth was, in fact, actually involved in a much cleverer game than perhaps it first appeared. Claiming not to remember, and being quite convincing about it, was quite a good strategy.

She was no match for Anderton though. He smiled with deceptive courtesy and said, "So you do admit to knowing Ali Araya better than at first you thought?"

Ruth was silent for a long moment. Then she gave

a very tiny nod. "I did know him, obviously I knew him, but we weren't close or anything like that. We weren't friends."

"Weren't you?" Anderton asked mildly.

"No."

Anderton glanced over at Kate, who indicated by a mere twitch of her eyebrows that he should go ahead with what she was sure he was going to ask. "What would you say, Ruth, if I told you we had it on good authority that you and Ali Araya had engaged in a sexual relationship?"

Ruth said nothing but she couldn't disguise the look of shock that briefly illuminated her face, or the burning flush that eclipsed its whiteness. She raised a hand to her hot cheek, inadvertently further drawing attention to it. "That's not true," she said, in the same small voice.

"Isn't it?"

Ruth said nothing.

Anderton went on, still in that gentle voice. "So you deny that you and Ali Araya were sexually involved? Because if that were the case, that would mean you did know him rather more intimately than you've told us, wouldn't it? That would mean that you and Ali were quite emotionally and physically intimate with one another?"

Ruth went to open her mouth but looked at her solicitor, who gave her a tiny shake of the head. Ruth closed her mouth again. She was hugging her arms tightly across her body; classic defensive behaviour, thought Kate.

Anderton let the silence run its course. Then he said, "Having a relationship with someone isn't against the law, Ruth. Even if you had been involved with Ali, why would you want to keep that a secret? Why does it matter?"

Ruth gave a single dry sob and raised her hand to her eyes. Anderton waited. Ruth put down her hand and sighed. She looked straight at Anderton. "He was very gentle. He was a very gentle person, I thought that was strange, given how much violence and pain he'd been exposed to, but perhaps that was why. He was reacting against all the chaos in his past."

"This is Ali we're talking about?" checked Anderton.

Ruth nodded. A flicker of pain and something close to—could it be?—cynicism crossed her face. "We never ran out of things to talk about. It made such a difference to have someone I could actually talk to." Tears filled her eyes and overflowed. Kate pushed the box of tissues on the table forward and Ruth pulled one from the box. "Thank you."

Suddenly, Kate ached with pity for her. She tried to imagine Ruth attacking the man who she seemed to have loved and found it difficult to picture. Was it possible? Ruth was tall but thin and didn't seem very physically strong. But Ali had not been a particularly big man... Kate dismissed the mental picture and turned her attention back to what Ruth was saying.

"We only slept together once. Perhaps it would have happened again, I don't know. We were attracted to one another but..." The colour had come back up into her cheeks again. She looked at Kate and then at Anderton in turn. "I'm sorry I didn't say so at the start. I was—I was embarrassed and I was fright—" She stopped speaking abruptly.

"Frightened?" asked Kate.

Ruth stared down at the table top again, her lips clamped together. She was very faintly shaking.

"Why would you be frightened, Ruth? Of the police?" Even as she asked the question, she could tell it was the wrong one. "Who frightens you?"

Ruth remained silent. Kate turned to Anderton and asked, "Sir, could I have a quick word outside?"

"Of course." Anderton suspended the interview and they went out into the corridor. "What's up?"

Kate hit herself on the forehead with her palm. "I can't believe I've been so stupid. I noticed a bruise on Ruth's throat the other day, and if I'm not mistaken, she might have a cigarette burn on her arm." She watched comprehension dawn on Anderton's face.

"Domestic violence?" was all he said.

"A definite possibility, don't you think? Should I run a background check on her boyfriend, Josh Beckett?"

"Yes. Do that. I'll carry on here but I think you might be onto something. That would explain why she was so reluctant to admit to the affair with Araya."

Kate nodded and began to head for the stairs. She heard Anderton call her back.

"Yes?" she asked.

Anderton looked serious. "Of course, if this is the case, it gives her another motive."

Kate hadn't thought that one through. She nodded, after a moment. "Oh God, it does too, doesn't it? If she was terrified of her boyfriend finding out..."

"Or perhaps Ali had threatened to reveal all to Josh..."

They looked at one another for a moment. Then Anderton shrugged. "Go and see what you can find on the boyfriend, if anything. Then we'll proceed from there."

Chapter Fourteen

"ANNE, COULD YOU DO SOMETHING for me?"

Anne looked enquiringly at Kate. "What is it that you want?"

"A background check on Joshua Beckett." Kate gave her the address of Ruth's flat. "Quick as you can, that would be great."

Anne bent to her work. Feeling a little pulse of gratitude that the donkey work was now someone else's to do, Kate stood for a moment in the middle of the office, slightly at a loss as to what to do next. Pondering, she made herself and Anne a cup of coffee and then sat back down at her desk. She checked her phone, realising Tin had sent her several photos: a montage of him posed in front of several London landmarks such as the Eye and Tower Bridge. She felt a little ache at the thought that it would be another couple of days until he was back in Abbeyford.

Anne was a fast and efficient worker. In less than twenty minutes, she had placed a number of printed reports in front of Kate.

"Oh, thanks so much." Kate quickly skimmed the first page. She clenched her fist in triumph. "Ah, I *knew* it."

Anne, who clearly wasn't up to speed on where the case was going, looked a bit puzzled. Kate thanked her again and got up, hurrying over to where Theo sat. "Fancy coming out with me to bring someone in?"

Theo flung an arm out in a dramatic gesture. "For you, Kate, I will walk to the ends of the Earth." Kate punched him on the arm. "Ow! What did I do?"

"Come on," Kate said. "I need a bloke with me, just in case."

"What's going on?"

"I'll tell you on the way. Come on, I'm driving."

"So," Theo said, perusing the printed notes as Kate drove to Salterton. "Convictions for assault, convictions for domestic abuse. What a catch."

"He's good looking enough," said Kate. "Perhaps that was the only attraction." She thought back to Ruth's flat, how Joshua Beckett had seemed out of place there. Why had Ruth taken up with him? She thought about all the clever, successful, compassionate women out there, living with and married to violent, abusive men. Why did they do it? For a moment she recalled her mother, and all the mistakes she'd made with men, and sighed.

The golden promise of the morning's weather had been kept. Now, in late afternoon, it was actually warm, summer's last gasp before winter made its appearance. Kate had to put her sunglasses on to cope with the glare as she drove along the seafront at Salterton.

Just as Kate was pulling into the kerb, her mobile rang. Theo answered it.

It was Anderton. Theo handed over the phone to Kate, who took it with a vague feeling of apprehension. Had Anderton got a confession already?

"Kate, it's me. Are you going to pick up Joshua Beckett?"

"Yes," Kate said with a qualm. Had she done the wrong thing? But Anderton had asked her to, hadn't he?

His next words soothed her. "Good. We're releasing Ruth Granger this evening." Kate must have made some sort of noise that Anderton interpreted as a protest. "I know, but we don't have the evidence to charge her with anything. I still think she's keeping something back, and we'll probably have to bring her in again, but unless something else comes to light, she's out for the moment."

"Okay." Kate looked over at Theo, who was listening in, and mouthed, 'Ruth Granger is being released'. Theo raised his eyebrows.

"Bring Joshua Beckett in now and we can make sure they don't have another opportunity to confer on anything."

"Right," Kate said. "Hopefully he'll come quietly."

"Have you got someone there with you?" Anderton

asked. He sounded worried, and Kate felt a jab of pleasure that came from knowing he was concerned for her. Then she stamped down hard on the feeling, feeling guilty.

"Theo's with me."

"Good. See you later."

"So, Ruth Granger's a no-go?" Theo asked as they got out of the car.

"Well, she's still a person of interest. But what have we really got on her? She lied about not knowing Ali Araya, at first, but she's admitted to an affair with him. What else have we got? She's got motive, all right, but where's the evidence to prove it?"

"Nowhere, so far," Theo said gloomily, as they walked up the path to Ruth Granger's flat.

*

JOSHUA BECKETT LOOKED MORE AT home in the interview room than his girlfriend had. He sat slumped, but relaxed, across the table from Theo and Kate. He looked an unlikely abuser. He had a face that would have been called pretty if he were a woman – chiselled jaw, rosebud lips, high cheekbones – but Kate could also see that beneath his grey sweatshirt top, his arms were corded with muscle. But then so often people didn't fit the stereotypes, did they? Kate turned her attention back to the notes in the notebook she laid on the table.

Beckett had refused a solicitor. Kate wondered

why. She decided to ask him, yet again, if he required legal representation.

"I'm all right," Beckett said with a scowl.

"Very well." Kate glanced across at Theo, knowing that he liked to take the lead. He inclined his head slightly, indicating that she should proceed.

"Mr Beckett, can you confirm your whereabouts on the night of the second of October, between the hours of eleven pm and four am?"

"I was at home. With Ruth."

"You didn't leave the flat at all at any time?"

Beckett's gaze shifted a little. "No."

Kate checked her notes again. "Did you know Ali Araya?"

"No."

"But you know who he was?"

"I'm not stupid." Beckett shifted in his seat, spreading his legs a little wider apart. "He's the bloke that got murdered on the beach. Ruth told me."

"So you yourself had no contact with him at any time?"

"No."

Kate cleared her throat. Not wanting to put Ruth into any kind of danger, she knew she had to tread carefully with the next couple of questions. "What was the relationship between your partner and Ali Araya?"

Beckett frowned. "What do you mean? They didn't have a relationship. She just knew him from the centre."

"Okay." Kate decided not to push any further. "So Ruth can confirm that you were at the flat, during the hours I've mentioned, on the night of the second of October? Did you see or speak to anyone else during that time?"

"No. It was just me and Ruth." He stared her directly in the eye, and she thought then *you're lying*. Everyone thought that the direct stare made your words sound truthful. It didn't.

They needed some way of proving his honesty, though. She made a note on her writing pad. *Check CCTV.*

Whilst she was writing, Theo continued the questions. "You have convictions for violent assault and domestic abuse, Joshua. Are you abusive to Ruth?"

A bit bald, Kate thought. Beckett scowled. "Has she said that? No, I'm not." Another direct stare into Theo's face. "All that stuff was a long time ago, right?"

Theo looked sceptical. "So, if we checked Ruth's medical records, possibly for hospital visits, stuff like that—we wouldn't find anything that might look suspicious?"

Beckett said nothing, still scowling ferociously. Theo said, "I see," and made his own notes on a writing pad.

"Did you know Nada Qabbani?" asked Kate.

This time Beckett stared blankly. "No," he said, eventually.

Kate could have sworn that the name meant

nothing to him. "You've never heard of the name or the person?"

"No. Never."

Much as she'd believed he was lying about the night of Ali Araya's death, Kate believed him when he said he hadn't known Nada. She was starting to think that this was all a waste of time.

After half an hour, they suspended the interview and left Beckett in the room with a cup of tea and a couple of biscuits. Kate shut the door and leant against it, looking up at Theo.

"What do you think?" she asked, speaking quietly so they wouldn't be overheard.

Theo shrugged. "He could be involved in the death of Ali Araya. But I don't think he's got anything to do with killing Nada Qabbani."

"Yes, I agree." Kate balled a fist in frustration. "God, we're getting nowhere fast. I'm going to see if there's anything on CCTV that can prove he wasn't at the flat on the night of Ali's murder."

"Okay," agreed Theo. "Look, I'll carry on here. Bring me anything you find and we'll see if that can break him down."

Kate climbed the stairs back up to the office, thinking hard. If Joshua Beckett hadn't known about Ruth's affair with Ali, and it sounded as though it would be news to him, then where was his motive for killing Ali? How could they prove that he had left Ruth's flat on the night of the murder? A further thought struck her and she stood still for a moment, staring blankly into space. Was Ruth alibiing Joshua, or was he alibiing Ruth? Or did neither of them have anything to do with it? Kate made a noise of frustration and began climbing again.

She called Chloe and requested any relevant CCTV footage from the night of Ali Araya's death. "Anything that might show either Joshua Beckett or Ruth Granger out and about."

"Leave it with me," Chloe suggested. "It'll be tomorrow morning, though."

"No problem," Kate said with an inner sigh. She looked at the clock, with the hands pointing to quarter past seven pm. It was long past the time she should have left. She said goodbye to Chloe, trailed back downstairs to inform Theo, and went to pack up her desk for the night.

Perhaps tomorrow would be more productive. Kate shut down her computer, feeling depressed. There came a point in every investigation, and this was no exception, where every lead seemed to point directly to a dead end. They still had no motive, no murder weapon, and the list of suspects seemed to be getting thinner by the day. *To hell with it*. Kate wanted a takeaway, a hot bath and a cuddle with Merlin. Perhaps that would make everything seem more worthwhile. It's worth a try anyway, she thought, closing the office door behind her as she left.

Chapter Fifteen

KATE WAS SIPPING HER THIRD cup of coffee the next morning, wondering when Chloe would send over the CCTV footage, when Rav bounded up to her desk, making her jump.

"Sorry," he said. "I just thought you might like to know that I've come from the PM on Nada Qabbani."

That got Kate's attention. She swung around to face him, eyebrows raised. "And?"

"You can rule out suicide. Gatkiss found out that she'd died several hours before midnight, apparently. Those injuries from the fall were all post-mortem."

Kate put her cup down, shaken. "My God. So it was murder."

"Looks that way," agreed Rav.

"Anything else come up? Does he know how she was killed?"

"No. There's no way of telling, given the state of her, poor woman. Unless she was poisoned, or something like that, but we'll have to wait for the tox tests to come back."

Kate was silent. Something had just occurred to her. "I've just realised. The MO in both cases is the same."

"What do you mean?"

Kate jumped up. "Come with me for a sec." She led him over to Olbeck's office, where the door was open. Kate knocked on the glass wall for courtesy.

"Come on in." Olbeck was poring over a stack of reports. Kate and Rav sat down on the chairs by his desk. "What's up?"

"Rav, tell him about the PM."

Rav did so. Olbeck raised his eyebrows but said nothing, only nodded.

Kate leant forward. "I was just telling Rav, I've just realised. There's a similarity between the cases, despite the method being different."

"Which is?" asked Olbeck.

"Both deaths were supposed to look like something other than murder." Kate held up a finger. "Ali Araya's death was supposed to look like an innocent drowning. You know, I think that's why the murderer dressed him in those clothes. We were supposed to think what we *did* at first think, which was he was an illegal immigrant, a refugee, trying to get to shore and drowning in the attempt."

"Right," said Olbeck. "That makes sense."

Kate held up the finger of her other hand. "Nada Qabbani's death *could* have been a suicide. Or an accident. Or so we were supposed to think. It's a pretty effective means of covering up injuries, isn't it? Hurling the body off the cliff so it smashes to bits on the ground. Not much chance of finding out she died from head injuries, or even strangulation or something like that."

"Yeah," Rav said with feeling. Olbeck gave him a sympathetic glance.

Kate went on. "The murderer is someone who wants to get away with it. We're not going to get someone breaking down and confessing, are we? Not realistically. Or handing themselves in."

"Unlikely," Olbeck agreed. "Unfortunately."

Kate put her hands back in her lap. Olbeck was jiggling his leg as he thought.

"There's a whole heap of second-hand clothes at the refugee centre," he said. "Someone could have swiped the ones we found Ali Araya wearing without anyone noticing."

"Yes." Kate had been thinking that herself.

At that moment, Anne put her head around the door. "Kate, there's a phone call for you. Bill Osbourne."

"Bill?" Kate was surprised. Bill Osbourne was one of the uniformed sergeants. It wasn't often that their paths collided.

She excused herself, leaving Rav and Olbeck talking, and went to her desk.

"Hi, Bill. It's Kate here."

"Morning, Kate. You've been interviewing Joshua Beckett, haven't you?"

Kate propped herself against her desk, frowning. "We were. He got released last night."

"Aye, I know. Bloke we pulled in ran into him at the station when he was leaving. Had something to say that you might find interesting."

"Really?" Kate started hunting for her notebook. "Who's this bloke?"

"Small time dealer, Alex Thomas. You'll recognise him. Anyway, given what he said about dates and timings, I think you should have a quick word with him before we bail him."

"Okay." Kate ascertained the cell number of Alex Thomas and then said thanks and goodbye to Bill. She put the phone down, wondering whether she should ask one of the others to accompany her. Olbeck and Rav were still deep in conversation. Kate shrugged to herself and hurried towards the stairs that led to the cell block floor.

As it happened, she *did* recognise Alex Thomas. He was one of the small band of petty criminals even an affluent town like Abbeyford couldn't escape; a scruffy, skinny man dressed in knock-off designer sportswear and sporting a cheap gold ring through his right eyebrow. He didn't seem to recognise her, though; perhaps unsurprisingly, given his daily ingestion of crappy drugs and cheap lager.

"Alex, I hear you have some information for us regarding Joshua Beckett?"

"Yeah," Thomas said, almost breezily. Like most

153

people used to the inside of a police station, he appeared quite relaxed. Such a contrast to Ruth Granger, Kate thought, remembering how stiffly the woman had sat, the tightness in her face.

"So, what is it that you have to tell me?"

"Well, it's like this, innit." Alex glanced across to where one of the uniformed officers was stationed by the door. PC Boulton stared back at him impassively. "Well, right, that night that bloke got killed, the black bloke. The one on the beach. Right?"

"Right," said Kate.

"Well, I hears that you're fitting Josh up for it. And that ain't right, because he can't have done it."

"When you say 'fitting' him up for it—" Kate began, trying to keep the sarcasm from her voice. From the sounds of it, the criminal grapevine was working just fine.

"Yeah. Well, he's a mate of mine and the thing is, right, is like he was with me that night."

"With you?"

She'd thought her tone was fairly neutral but Thomas flushed angrily. "Not like that, right? You lot are dirty fuckers, you know that?"

Kate repressed the urge to wash his mouth out with soap. "Alex, do you actually have anything to tell us or not? You're saying Joshua Beckett was with you on the night of Ali Araya's death? From what time to what time?"

Thomas had calmed down a little. He fiddled with

the ring in his eyebrow. "Dunno, exactly. But he came over sometime that night, to get some gear, right. And then we stayed up, right, like, most of the night. He only left when it was daytime again."

"What were you doing all night?" Kate asked, unsure of how else to phrase it but hoping that he wouldn't bridle up again. "Apart from taking drugs, of course."

This time Thomas remained calm. He looked unembarrassed. "Mostly playing WoW. Got up to the next level, fuck yeah."

"What?"

He gave her a contemptuous look. "World of Warcraft, innit."

Kate just about knew that that was a computer game. She looked down at the hasty notes she'd scribbled. Alex Thomas had been arrested for intent to supply and, with his previous record, was probably looking at a prison sentence.

"Why tell us this now?"

Thomas looked virtuous. "Well, he's a mate, innit. I don't want 'im to go down for murder, do I? Thought it'd be better 'im being done for a little bit of gear than getting locked down in the slammer for fourteen plus, yeah?" Kate must have looked unconvinced because he went on, in a more triumphant tone "And that'll get me a reduction on me sentence, right? Giving evidence an' that."

Kate burst out laughing. "This isn't 'LA Law', you

know." She got up to go. "I'll get someone to come and take your statement, Alex."

"Wait, they're gonna take it into account, yeah? On my sentencing?" Thomas looked panicked.

Kate fought to keep a straight face. "We'll see what we can do." She exchanged an eloquent glance with an expressionless PC Boulton and left the interview room.

As Kate climbed the stairs back to the office, she could feel the smile dropping off her face. If what Alex Thomas said was true, and she saw no reason to doubt him, junkie fool that he was, then Joshua Beckett was in the clear. He had clearly lied about being at home with Ruth the night of Ali Araya's murder because he feared arrest for drug taking and buying. But what did that mean for Ruth? If Joshua hadn't been at home with her, why had *she* lied? Kate walked into the office, frowning. She went straight to Olbeck's office, where he was typing busily. Rav was back at his desk, flipping through a pile of reports.

Kate told Olbeck what she'd just found out.

"Okay." Olbeck looked troubled. "I'm sure you'll have worked out the problem here."

"Problem for Ruth, you mean. Not for us."

"Exactly. If Alex Thomas is telling the truth—"

"I think he is," said Kate. "He doesn't have the wit to lie about it."

"Well, then, if it's true, Joshua Beckett is in the clear. And Ruth's alibi is smashed to pieces."

"I know."

They looked at each other across the desk.

"I'm going to run this past Anderton," Olbeck said, getting up. "Then we're pulling Ruth Granger in again for another talk."

Chapter Sixteen

RUTH GRANGER LOOKED NO MORE at home in the interview room than she had the first time. This time, she wore a thick, knitted sweater, the sleeves of which she kept pulling down over her wrists, and her grey hair was loose around her face. It looked greasy and unwashed, and her face was not made up. She looked as though she hadn't slept in a week.

Kate and Olbeck seated themselves opposite Ruth and the duty solicitor, one of the older men from the local practice. He was one of three solicitors that Kate always found rather hard to tell apart because they all seemed to have the same side-parted grey hair, heavy tortoiseshell rimmed spectacles, and wore identical grey suits with blue-striped ties.

Kate had made sure Ruth had a cup of tea before they started, and she had discreetly ensured that there was a box of tissues within reaching distance. She had a feeling they would probably be needed.

"Ruth, when we spoke before, you said that you and Joshua spent the night of the second of October at home, just the two of you." Kate paused for a beat. "Do you wish to amend that part of your statement?"

Ruth gave her a quick, scared look. "No," she said, after a moment's pause.

"Are you sure?"

Ruth said nothing.

Kate shuffled her papers. "Ruth, we have a witness who can place Joshua with him during most of the night of the second October, the night of Ali Araya's death. What do you say to that?"

Ruth still said nothing. She stared intently at the table top. Kate wondered whether she was doing it to stop the tears from forming in her eyes.

"I'll ask again, what really happened on that night? Why did you say Joshua was with you when he wasn't?"

Still nothing from Ruth. Kate could see the solicitor observing his client keenly and wondered whether he would step in. She pressed on regardless.

"The way I see it, Ruth, is that there are two possibilities as to why you lied to us about that night." Ruth flinched slightly at the word lie. "That is, you lied because you knew Joshua had gone out and you were worried he might get into trouble." She was watching Ruth's face, watching the emotions flicker through her before being quickly suppressed. "Perhaps you lied because you were worried that he actually had something to do with Ali's death." Ruth's face twitched but she still said nothing.

Kate persisted. "Are you frightened of your boyfriend, Ruth?" The duty solicitor shifted in his seat, and Kate hurried on before he could speak. "He has convictions for violent assault and domestic abuse. I assume you were aware of this?"

Ruth's face grew even whiter. She didn't know, Kate thought. She thought it was just her he was doing those things to.

"Did you know that about Joshua?"

After a moment, Ruth shook her head. "No," she said hoarsely.

Kate sat back a little, letting the other woman absorb the news. Olbeck suggested a short break for tea, with which Kate concurred.

As they fetched the drinks, leaving Ruth and her solicitor in the interview room, Kate caught at Olbeck's arm. "Is it worth pushing the abuse angle further?"

Olbeck shrugged. "Up to you. I notice you haven't mentioned the second possibility."

"I'm saving that for last," said Kate. She picked up two plastic cups, and Olbeck took the other two. As they walked back, trying not to spill anything, she found herself unaccountably reluctant. It was the thought of what she was going to say to Ruth. It seemed brutal.

Come on, you're a police officer. Pull yourself together.

Once they were all seated, Kate marshalled her thoughts. The solicitor was sipping gingerly at his plastic cup of tea but Ruth hadn't touched hers.

"I'm sorry," Kate apologised. "It's not very good tea but at least it's hot."

Ruth stared down at the table top again. "I'll have it in a minute," she said in what was almost a whisper.

Kate sat up in her seat. "So, Ruth, how did you and Joshua meet?" She'd decided to go off on a tangent for a moment, see what came up. "Have you been together long?"

Ruth looked at her for a moment, clearly wondering where this was leading. "About a year," she said cautiously.

"How did you meet?"

Ruth finally reached out and picked up her tea. The warmth of it in her hands seemed to comfort her and calm her down a little. She clasped it in both hands. "I was travelling. We met in India and started travelling together. When we came back to England, well, he didn't have a job, and it seemed the right thing to do to move in together..." She trailed off, clearly wondering at her earlier decision.

"Ruth," Kate said softly, leaning forward. "Is he violent towards you? I've noticed bruises, things like that, on you..."

Ruth's face tightened and she put the cup down.

"You haven't done anything wrong," Kate said, hoping that was true. "It's not your fault if he abuses you. It can be hard to admit but there's plenty of help to be had."

Again, there was nothing. Silence. Kate felt Olbeck's

foot press against hers under the table. She was pierced by the memory of doing that to Anderton, years ago, directly after their very brief affair. Quickly, she recollected herself. *Sorry, Ruth, you leave me no choice...*

"Ruth, as I've said before, you have repeatedly lied to us about either yours or Joshua's whereabouts on the night Ali Araya was murdered. What really happened?"

Silence.

Kate repressed a sigh. "Where were you on the night before last, the night Nada Qabbani was killed?"

That got a response. Ruth's heavily shadowed eyes widened. "Killed? Nada was killed? I thought she jumped."

"That knowledge hasn't been made public yet," Kate said, watching her keenly. "What did you do after I left you at the refugee centre that night?"

Ruth reached for her tea, realised everyone could see her shaking fingers, and swiftly withdrew her hand. "Nada was killed?" She shut her eyes. "Oh my god, this is just a nightmare. A nightmare..." Her voice cracked, and she put a hand up to her mouth to hide her trembling lips.

Kate watched. "Where were you, Ruth?"

Ruth opened her eyes and lowered her hand. She suddenly looked spent, as if all the energy had just run out of her. Kate had seen this in suspects before, and she braced herself. It was normally just before they decided they couldn't keep a secret any longer. Was she going to confess? She could tell by Olbeck's sudden tautness beside her that he was thinking the same thing. But then she remembered her own words to him, earlier in the day. *The murderer is someone who wants to get away with it. We're not going to get someone breaking down and confessing...*

"I was very upset that night," Ruth said in a low voice. "I'd had—I'd had an awful row with Josh and I was... I was very upset. I didn't want to go home."

Kate waited but it appeared Ruth had stopped speaking. "And?" She prompted.

Ruth cleared her throat. "If you must know, I went to a pub for a drink."

"On your own?"

"Yes. I was—I was feeling so low I just didn't want to be with anyone, and I knew if I went home, Josh would—would start—" She broke off, hanging her head. Kate saw a tear fall into her lap.

Despite herself, Kate felt pity. "Which pub was this?"

"The Jolly Sailor. On the front."

Ruth's presence there that night should be easy to check, what with identification and CCTV. "Did you see or speak to Nada Qabbani at all that evening?"

Ruth shook her head. "No. I didn't even know she was there."

"Know she was there? Where?"

Ruth looked confused. "At the refugee centre." She looked frightened suddenly. "I mean, I don't know she was there, I just assumed by the way you said it..."

Kate let her stutter into silence. Then she spoke. "Ruth, I'd said that there were two possibilities as to why you lied about your whereabouts on the night of Ali Araya's death. The first, as I've said, is that you could have been falsely alibi-ing your boyfriend, because you were frightened of him getting into trouble with the police, either because of what he was actually doing or because you thought he might have had something to do with Ali Araya's death." She waited for Ruth to comment, but the woman simply sat there, stony-faced. Kate continued. "I haven't mentioned the second possibility."

Ruth looked up and the duty solicitor suddenly became alert.

Kate went on. "The second possibility is that you falsely claimed you and Joshua were at home together that night because you were providing an alibi for yourself."

Ruth looked at her with horror. Kate wondered whether it was the first time it had sunk in, that she, Ruth herself, was suspected of the murder of Ali Araya.

"Where were you really that night, Ruth?"

Ruth tried to speak through what was obviously a bone-dry throat. She swallowed painfully and tried again. "I was at home. All night. I promise you I'm telling the truth. I admit I lied about Josh because I was afraid—just like you said, I was afraid he might have—have found out about Ali and me and he'd hurt him. But I wasn't—I didn't go anywhere, I had nothing to do with it."

Kate nodded, letting the other woman talk her way down to silence. Then she decided to fire a few more questions her way. "Was Ali Araya blackmailing you, Ruth?"

"What?"

"Was he blackmailing you? Had he found out something about you that you needed to be kept quiet?"

Ruth was staring at her with what looked like a mixture of horror and surprise. "What? I don't understand what you mean."

"Why would Ali Araya have said, about you, that you're not what you seem?"

By now Ruth was in a state of total incomprehension. "I—I don't know what you mean. I never heard Ali say that."

"You wouldn't have heard him. He mentioned it to someone else."

Ruth raised both hands to her temples, pressing inwards. Her eyes closed, as if in pain.

"I think my client might need another break," suggested the solicitor.

"In a minute," Kate said, unmoved. She leant forward. "What would Ali mean by that, Ruth?"

"I don't know!" Ruth sounded on the verge of tears. "There's nothing—the only thing I didn't want to come out was the fact we'd—we'd had a relationship.

Because I was bloody terrified of Joshua finding out. And that's all." She was crying freely now. "I—I didn't hurt Ali, I wasn't anywhere but home that night. You—you have to believe me."

Kate sat back in silence. The room was filled with wet sounds of Ruth's sobs.

"I don't—I don't understand what's happening," Ruth gasped, her face buried in her hands. Her grey hair shone under the ceiling light, despite the grease. "Nothing makes sense anymore, nothing. If it was just the money, even that doesn't make sense, but now it's everything, it's death—I—I can't—" She became incoherent, bending forward and shuddering.

"I think we'll take a short break," Olbeck said and spoke the words to indicate a pause in the proceedings.

Chapter Seventeen

DURING THEIR SHORT BREAK, KATE headed back to her desk to check her emails. She saw she'd missed a call from Chloe while she was in the interview.

"Listen," she said to Olbeck, as he walked past her desk towards the office door. "Can you carry on without me? I've got to check in with Salterton."

"Sure. If they've got anything that might substantiate Ruth's claim, that she was home all night, then let me have it ASAP."

"Will do." Kate gave him a wave as he hurried away, thinking it was probably more likely that CCTV would negate Ruth's alibi. If there was any footage of her on the streets of Salterton during those crucial hours on the night of Ali Araya's death, then Ruth was lying, pure and simple.

Kate dialled Chloe's number. "Sorry I missed you."

Chloe sounded rather harried. "Look, I've managed to get some footage of that night. There's quite a lot to go through—I didn't realise how many cameras Salterton actually had. It's quite frightening, in a civil liberties sort of way."

"So, anything that might help?"

"Well, yes, in a way. There's clear footage of Joshua Beckett entering the road on which Alex Thomas lives, and the times tally with the information we were given."

"Right." Kate scribbled a few notes. "So, evidence-wise, we're going to struggle to prove that he was anywhere near Muddiford Beach at the crucial hours."

"Yes. Especially as he isn't seen leaving until about five am the next morning."

"Right." Kate wrote Joshua Beckett on her notepad and put a thick black line through it. "Well, he's out. What about Ruth?" She held her breath, wondering whether she'd have something crucial to relay to Olbeck.

Chloe sounded regretful. "No, no there's nothing that I could see."

Kate exhaled. Sometimes, she thought, it would be nice if the universe could give you just one break. "Great. So she's out then, too?"

She could almost hear Chloe shrug. "Look, there's still hours of footage to go through but I've checked it from the nearest point to Ruth's flat, the way to Muddiford and all around the refugee centre and she can't be seen anywhere there." Kate made a noise of frustration. "Yeah, I know. Listen, I'll get the analysts to email over the footage of Beckett, but there's something else I thought you might want to be in on. We're searching Nada Qabbani's rooms first thing tomorrow. Nine am, if you want to come."

"Yes," Kate said immediately. "I'll be there. What's the address?"

After she'd put the phone down, Kate hesitated, unsure as to whether to re-join Olbeck in the interview room or to get on with looking through the CCTV footage that—she saw the arrival notification of the email pop up as she was thinking—Salterton had just sent through. In the end, she scribbled a note for Olbeck: *no CCTV footage of Ruth on night of 2nd Oct as yet but am going to double check. Joshua Beckett story re. Alex Thomas seems legit. K.*

She ran down to the interview room, knocked, entered, and handed it over. Ruth Granger had stopped crying but her eyes looked red-raw under the harsh strip light. There was another steaming, untouched cup of tea in front of her. Kate had to stamp down on another jab of pity.

She hurried back upstairs to her desk and opened the email from Salterton. Chloe had helpfully marked the files that contained the footage that she'd already checked. Privately, Kate decided she'd view them herself—it wasn't that she didn't trust Chloe but it was always helpful to have a fresh pair of eyes on the footage, just in case something had been missed. But she might as well start with the films that hadn't been viewed. Unbidden, Anne put a mug of tea in front of her and Kate thanked her effusively.

It was boring, tedious work and, after a couple of hours, she was glad of the excuse to stop for a break. She had heard her mobile chime with an incoming text message and she pulled it from her handbag, noting with pleasure that it was Tin texting her. He'd written, *Hi sweetheart, can you give me a call when you get this? Thanx.*

Kate got up, stretched and headed for the exit. She'd grab five minutes of fresh air while she talked to her boyfriend; kill two birds with one stone.

Outside, she went around the back of the station to the smoking area, not her first choice of location but at least there were some benches there to sit on and the odd bit of greenery. The ground was thick with dead leaves and Kate had to walk carefully to keep from slipping.

"Hello, sweets," said Tin as he answered the phone. Kate could hear traffic in the background, sirens, the usual buzz and hum of London going about its business. She gave a silent prayer of thanks that she didn't have to work there.

"How's it going?"

"Fine." Tin sounded—well, a little odd. Not upset, not angry—just not quite his usual cheerful self.

"Are you okay?"

"Fine. I'm fine. How's things with you?"

Kate gave him a potted history of what she'd been

up to over the past few days. She finished by saying how much she was looking forward to seeing him that night when he got back to Abbeyford.

"Ah," Tin said, sounding uneasy. "About that. Listen, something's come up, and I have to stay up here for a couple of days."

"Really?" Kate could hear the disappointment in her tone. Not only that, she was aware of a little pulse of disquiet. "Why is that?"

"Oh, it's nothing much. Just a couple of meetings." Now Tin definitely sounded cagey. "I can't say much more at the moment."

"Why can't you?" demanded Kate.

"Because—look, it's all a bit up in the air at the moment. That's all I can tell you."

"What is?" There was a pause on the other end of the line over which Kate could hear what sounded like a ferry boat horn sound. "Where *are* you?"

"On the South Bank." That explained the river noises, thought Kate. "Look, it's nothing dodgy," Tin continued, sounding dodgier than ever.

Kate was battling against a paranoid fantasy that Tin was about to leave her for another woman, some London sophisticate who wore designer suits (in her mind's eye, Kate could picture this femme fatale, looking oddly like the blonde lawyer Anderton used to go out with). Tin was saying something else, but Kate barely heard him, taken up with jealous visions as she was.

"So it just means that I have to have this meeting with him the day after tomorrow," Tin was saying.

Kate dragged herself back to reality. "Who's 'him'?"

"The editor," Tin said patiently.

Kate knew of Tin's editor. "What, Peter?"

"No," said Tin, sounding more impatient. "That's what I've been trying to tell you. The editor at *The Independent*."

Now Kate was thoroughly lost. "What editor at The Independent?"

"Haven't you been listening? I said, I've got a meeting with the editor at the Indie because there's a potential job offer in the making. That's why I've got to stay up here for another couple of days. But I can't say any more just yet."

Relieved that she wasn't being dumped unceremoniously—really, she shouldn't be so paranoid—Kate barely had time to wonder why there was so much secrecy involved. All she knew of newspaper publication was through Tin himself—perhaps this was normal. "So when will you be back?"

"In a few days, It depends whether it goes to second interviews or not, I suppose."

"Well, good luck," Kate said, feeling a bit flat. She'd been looking forward to seeing Tin. And there was something else too, something of the conversation they'd just had, that niggled. What had it been?

"Thanks. Listen, I'll try and call you later, okay? I've got to run. Love you."

"Love you," Kate said automatically. She heard Tin say goodbye and then hang up.

Frowning, Kate stood for a moment, ankle-deep in dead leaves. There was still something bothering her about what they'd just talked about, but for the life of her, she couldn't put her finger on what it was. Was it just that Tin had been so cagey about what he was doing? But then, he *had* told her he couldn't talk about it... Kate began to walk back towards the back door of the station, thinking hard. She felt another twinge of paranoia. Had Tin been telling her the truth? She had no reason to doubt him, none at all, but then...why this sudden sense of unease? Kate walked back into the welcome warmth of the station, frowning, her thoughts far from her current case.

She sat back down at her desk and tried to concentrate on what she was doing. Slowly, she worked her way through all the CCTV footage files, looking out for Ruth's distinctive hair and memorable face. Every so often, she found her thoughts straying back to Tin. There was something he'd said that made her uneasy, but *what*? What was it? Every time she tried to put her finger on it, it slid away like smoke through the air. *You're just worried because he's not telling you something.* Perhaps that was it.

It was past nine o'clock when Kate closed the last of the files. She'd found nothing to suggest that Ruth was anywhere other than where she'd said she'd been on the night of Ali Araya's death—her flat. Kate closed down her computer, yawning. With a guilty start, she realised Merlin was probably yowling for his food back at her own place. Quickly, she gathered up her things and hurried out to her car, locking the office door behind her.

Chapter Eighteen

KATE GOT UP THE NEXT morning feeling as though she hadn't slept. She'd had strange dreams, where she was walking with Tin along what she'd assumed her subconscious meant to be the South Bank, but in her sleeping mind, it had assumed giant and fantastical proportions. The River Thames had stretched for miles, the opposite bank almost lost in the distance. She and Tin had been looking for something but as Kate awoke, the sense of urgency she'd felt in her dreams receded sharply and she couldn't remember what it was they'd been looking for with such panic.

She was due to meet Chloe, and presumably a few of the other Salterton officers, at nine am. Groaning, she stumbled into the shower, dried and dressed and swallowed several cups of strong coffee. Merlin twined like a lithe black ribbon around her ankles as she did so.

"What's going on with Tin, my darling cat?" Kate asked him rhetorically. "What's he playing at?" Merlin gave her a short *miaow* in response, just as if he'd really understood her. She was still conscious of that little finger of unease. It was like a tiny knot in the pit of her stomach; minuscule but still irrefutably there. She sighed, bent down to rub Merlin behind his ears in farewell, and headed out of the door.

The weather didn't exactly help her mood. It was a grey blustery sort of day, and the autumn colours of the trees just looked dreary and untidy, like russet and orange paints that had been carelessly smeared together in an indifferent composition. Kate drove towards Salterton and towards the bedsit where Nada Qabbani had eaten and slept and mourned her dead.

Just thinking about that put Kate in a bad mood. She was further depressed to see the run-down old house where Nada had lived. Once it had probably been quite a grand Victorian residence; the outside of the three story house was covered in peeling paint, once white, now faded to a dirty cream. Several of the windowpanes were cracked and one was boarded up with what looked like cardboard. Black plastic bags of rubbish were stacked up in the basement area and the stink of decaying food was what greeted Kate as she walked up the short flight of stairs to the front door.

"What a dump," were her first words to Chloe. She thought of what Rav had said, about how the refugees were pushing aside British families who needed homes, and wondered if that were true. What family would want to live here, if they could help it?

Chloe was waiting at the front door with

another Salterton colleague, the 'fat old git', as Kate remembered Theo describing him. An accurate description, thought Kate, cynically amused. She'd forgotten the man's name and was grateful to Chloe for introducing him again as Detective Constable Harold Smith. Kate shook hands and promptly forgot his name again.

Not that it mattered. The three of them shuffled through the entrance into the hallway. Again, the bare bones of what had once been an imposing house shone through. The floor had been tiled in black and white tiles, like a chessboard, but some of these had been removed or had fallen apart and the gaps showed like missing teeth in a smile. Junk mail, dust and dead leaves were piled in every corner. The walls looked as though they had last been painted sometime around the turn of the century.

"Nada's room is along here, apparently," Chloe said, somewhat unnecessarily as they could all see the blue and white tape decorating a door further down the dark hallway. Chloe had the key to the room in her hand and she opened it, pushing it as it stuck. They all ducked under the tape and into the tiny room. Chloe reached for the light switch and turned the overhead light on, illuminating the room.

It was pathetically neat and clean, a contrast to the squalor outside, although a fine bloom of dust coated everything. There was barely anything in the room apart from a narrow single bed, a bedside table and another narrow gate-leg table, over by the far wall. Several cardboard boxes stacked against a wall had obviously served Nada as a makeshift wardrobe. A small suitcase could be seen under the bed. Was this all she had managed to bring from Syria? It seemed likely, given how quickly she said she had needed to flee. There were a couple of books on the flimsy bedside table and Kate, pulling on her gloves, went to lift them up. One was a copy of The Quran. Another seemed to be a novel, but as it was written in Arabic, Kate had no way of knowing what it was.

The three of them stood for a moment, regarding their dismal surroundings. Kate thought of Nada; she'd escaped almost certain death, lost her lover, lost her family. She'd ended up here, in a cold foreign country, with no money and no real home, clearly haunted by her past. And she'd made a friend, in Ali Araya, and then someone had killed him and then killed Nada because she knew too much, or the killer thought she knew too much. A life full of sorrow that ended in tragedy, and Kate didn't know why. She felt her fists clench.

DS Smith had already moved towards the cardboard boxes and was kneeling down before them, with some difficulty given his bulk. Chloe and Kate stood side by side in the middle of the minuscule room. It felt crowded with just three people in it.

"You know," Chloe said in a low voice. "You know what really grates? That some people have absolutely fuck all, and even then, some bastard takes it away from them."

She looked at Kate, who nodded fervently. "I was just thinking the same thing myself."

The two of them stood in a black fog for a moment. Then Chloe sighed and shook herself and moved towards the bed. "Come on. It shouldn't take us long."

In fact, it took an almost embarrassingly short time to search the room. There was barely anything to search. Kate and Chloe checked the bed, heaved up the thin mattress, felt underneath the springs. They looked for where the mattress itself might have been slit, to provide a discreet storage place, but there was nothing.

DS Smith had sorted through the small amount of clothes Nada had possessed and found nothing of interest. They checked the suitcase, which was empty of everything except some official papers confirming Nada had had her asylum claim accepted. There was also a purse containing what Kate assumed was Syrian currency in coins and notes. It didn't look very much.

After half an hour, the room had been thoroughly searched. Kate sat down on the edge of the bed and picked up the two books from the bedside table. She shook the pages of the Quran, and riffled through it in as respectful a manner as possible, before placing it gently back on the table. Then she did the same to the novel. A small, paper-wrapped package thumped to the floor.

Chloe and DS Smith had been conferring by the door in low voices. At Kate's exclamation, they turned sharply.

"What is it?" asked Chloe.

Kate was examining the inside of the book. A small cuboid shape had been cut from the pages of the book and the package had been concealed inside.

Chloe picked up the package with her gloved hands and carefully unwrapped it. A variety of expressions chased themselves across her face as what was inside was revealed.

"What is it?" It was Kate's turn to ask.

"It's an Apple watch." Chloe sounded blank. She smoothed the straps of the watch out on her palm.

Kate got up from the bed to look. DS Smith had also walked the three steps over from the door.

"An Apple watch?" Kate looked at the small black object in Chloe's hand. "But—they're quite expensive, aren't they?"

DS Smith extended one podgy hand and shot his shirt cuff back. There, strapped incongruously around his hairy, freckled wrist was a similar watch. "Paid about 300 quid for that one," he said, sounding rather proud. The two women looked at his watch for a moment and then back at the one found in Nada's book.

"Okay, that's weird," Chloe said abruptly. "Where would a penniless refugee get an Apple watch from?"

"Could she have brought it with her from Syria?" suggested Kate.

DS Smith scoffed. "As if! They only came out over here this year. I highly doubt Apple are shipping them to Damascus."

"All right," Kate said, a little stung. "So what's the explanation?"

They all looked at the watch again. Kate smoothed out the paper wrapping and realised something was written on it. She read it out, wonderingly. "'Insurance policy! Ali. X'"

They all regarded each other for a moment. "Ali Araya gave it to her?" Chloe said.

Kate read the message again. "Well, if that's his handwriting. Perhaps she knew another Ali... No, it doesn't seem likely, does it? It must have been Araya." She read it again. "'Insurance policy'? What the hell does that mean?"

"If Ali Araya gave it to Nada, then where did *he* get it?" Chloe sounded as though she were thinking aloud. "It's not as if he were flush with cash either, was he? Where the hell did he get it?"

"Nicked it," DS Smith speculated, lugubriously.

"Hmm." Chloe was staring at the watch as if its blank, black face was about to spring to life and tell her all its secrets. "It's possible. Are they registered to an owner?" She looked over at DS Smith with raised eyebrows. "Are they, Harold?"

"They can be. Not everyone does it, though."

"Well, that should be easy enough to check,"

Chloe said. She dropped the watch and the note into an evidence bag.

Kate was thinking. "Perhaps what Ali meant is that he or Nada could always sell it if they ever needed the money, do you think?"

"Maybe." Chloe didn't sound that convinced.

They continued to search but found nothing else of interest. Taking a last look round, Kate offered up a silent message to Nada's spirit, just in case she was there. *I'll do my best, Nada. I'll do my best.*

DS Smith said he had another appointment and said goodbye casually, waddling off down the street. Chloe and Kate paused for a moment on the top step, as Chloe locked the door to the house behind them.

"What are you up to now?" she asked Kate.

Kate blew out her cheeks. "I'll check on where we are with Ruth Granger. See if we've got a positive ID on her in the pub she says she was at the night Nada was killed. Um—" she thought, running through the checklist in her head. "See if anything else has come in."

"I'll check up on this watch, see if it's registered to anyone, get it fingerprinted."

They began to walk down the steps. Light spots of rain began to fall and Kate calculated how long it would take to dash to her car—she'd left her coat on the front seat.

"I'll let you know," said Chloe, obviously preparing to leave.

"Thanks." For a moment, despite the increasingly heavy rain, Kate stood irresolute. She wanted to tell Chloe about the increasing unease she was feeling, that they were all missing something important, that the key to the case was shimmering somewhere inside her consciousness but was unable to articulate what she felt.

Chloe had stopped and was looking at her. "What's wrong?" she asked.

She was a perceptive woman, Kate realised. She remembered Chloe telling her that, just before apologising for reading Kate wrong. There was something else that Chloe had said, about someone, that resonated with the way Kate was feeling now. Who had it been? What had Chloe said? It chimed in with the conversation she'd had with Tin, where something had been misunderstood. What *was* it?

The tantalising shimmer of an answer was there, just out of reach. Frustrated, Kate closed her eyes and screwed up her face.

"What is it?" asked Chloe, more urgently.

"I don't know," said Kate. Getting the words out was almost painful. "I think—I need to *think*. There's something I've heard or seen that—*argh*—is important but I just can't remember what it was..."

Chloe waited in silence for a moment. Then she

said, not unkindly, "Perhaps you need to stop trying so hard. Maybe you're blocking it out."

Kate let out her breath in a sigh. "Maybe you're right," she admitted. "Maybe it'll come to me if I let it."

She suddenly realised they were both standing in quite heavy rain. "Look, you go on." She tried to smile. "I'll call you if inspiration strikes."

Chloe grinned. "You do that. See you later."

They both parted, Kate dashing through the rain to her car. She flung herself into the driver's seat, raking her wet fringe out of her eyes. *Time for a haircut, Kate.* She blotted her wet face with her dry coat's sleeve and reached for the car keys in the ignition.

There was a chime as a text message came through on her mobile phone. Kate hesitated, wondering whether to leave it. Curiosity won out and she picked it up, realising it was from Tin. *Go me. Going to second interview. Meeting editor this afternoon but might be able to get back after that. Will call you later xx.*

Kate read it. Her eyes lingered on one word. Then she gave a cry as something clicked into place—she actually heard it, an audible clunk—and she grabbed up the phone, pressing the screen for Tin's mobile number.

"Hi," she said breathlessly, when he answered. "Listen—"

"Good news, huh? I wasn't sure whether they'd gone for me, to be honest, you know what interviews are like—"

"Tin, wait." Kate rushed to speak over him. "When we spoke the other day, do you remember? You said you were going to see your editor and I thought you meant Peter and you didn't? You actually meant someone else, but I misheard or got confused because you just used the word, do you remember?"

"What?" Tin sounded understandably confused.

"The other day, you said you were going to see your editor, and I thought you meant—" Kate stopped abruptly, realising she didn't need Tin to explain or even recall their conversation. She knew now why it had made her uneasy.

There was a baffled and somewhat offended silence on the other end of the line. Then Tin said, "Are you even going to say well done on getting through to the next round, or what?"

Kate was too struck with her revelation to feel more than a tiny burst of guilt. "Of course. Sorry, well done," she said, well aware of sounding perfunctory. "Sorry, darling, but I'm right in the middle of something here. I'll call you later and shower you with accolades. Seriously." She was joking, trying to lighten the mood. "When you get back we'll have champagne, I promise."

"Okay then," said Tin after a moment, still sounding huffy.

"Sorry," Kate said more sincerely. "You've done brilliantly. I'm sure you'll get the job."

"Okay."

"Love you. Got to go."

"Bye then." The phone went silent, but Kate was too excited by what she'd realised to worry too much. She flung the mobile on the passenger seat and started the car.

Then she turned it off. She realised she had to make one more call and dialled the number.

Chloe sounded as though she hadn't yet reached the station. Kate could hear the rain hissing down in the background.

"I've thought of something," Kate said, not beating around the bush. "But it's still too nebulous to do anything about, just yet. I need to do a bit of digging, but if I can find something that might stick, then I'm going to go up to London. Did you want to come?"

"Yes." Kate could hear Chloe wondering silently whether to ask her to go into more detail and was struck with admiration when the other woman obviously decided against it. That must mean she trusts me, thought Kate, feeling a warm glow at the thought.

"I'm going to go back now and pull up everything I can. It may take me more than a day but I'll let you know as soon as I can."

"Okay." Chloe sounded guarded, but underneath that, Kate thought she caught a glimpse of anticipation, maybe even excitement.

She said goodbye and started the drive back to Abbeyford. It was like this in every case, she thought. You thought you'd hit rock bottom, a standstill; there seemed to be obstacles at every turn. And then, suddenly, almost miraculously, something happened. A piece of evidence, a chance phrase that suddenly illuminated the darkness, the puzzle pieces slowly but inexorably dropping into place.

She parked her car in the underground car park at Abbeyford station, went to buy an extra-large, extra-strong coffee from the local greasy-spoon café and headed down to the basement and to the I.T. department, where she asked Sam for one of the office laptops. She had already decided not to sit at her desk—she wanted peace and quiet, an ability to concentrate without being distracted by tea runs, or Theo's banter, or Olbeck stopping for a chat. She had work to do.

Chapter Nineteen

KATE DREW UP OUTSIDE CHLOE'S house the next morning just as the weak rays of the autumn sun were beginning to finally strengthen into warmth. She opened the window, and took a deep breath of the briny air, before beeping her horn to warn Chloe that she'd arrived.

The front door soon opened and Chloe appeared. As usual she was dressed in one of her black suits, with a briefcase in one hand, her blonde hair twisted neatly back from her face. If it hadn't been for the brown paper bag in the other hand, she could have been off to her job on the trading floor, somewhere in the City of London.

"Morning," she said, opening the car door. An inviting smell came in with her, and Kate looked enquiringly at the paper bag. "Bacon sandwiches for the journey," explained Chloe.

"Oh, you star." Kate held out an eager hand. "I'm famished. Didn't even have time for breakfast."

"Tut-tut. Most important meal of the day." Chloe

settled herself into the passenger seat and dug in the bag for a sandwich. "Here you go."

"We'll stop for coffee too." Kate set off, driving gingerly with one hand as she scoffed the sandwich. "I want to hit London before the traffic gets too bad."

At this point in the morning, local traffic was light. They were soon out of Salterton and heading for the motorway.

"So," said Chloe. "What have you found?"

Kate swallowed the last mouthful of bacon with some regret. "It occurred to me, yesterday morning, that things can be so easily be misconstrued. Or misheard. And, if that's the case, then we could be barking up the wrong tree, as it were."

Chloe looked at her. "Meaning?"

Kate glanced over. "Wait, I hadn't finished. There was also something that Ruth said, that was forgotten about at the time. Just a quick comment and because she was upset and crying, it kind of got forgotten about. But after I remembered it, I thought—well, that needs looking into. Or at least, we need to think about what she might have meant."

"What did she say?"

Kate was negotiating her way onto the motorway and took a moment to answer. Once the car was safely ensconced in the middle lane, she spoke. "Ruth said something like 'it's not just the money that doesn't make sense' or something like that. And it was such a throwaway remark, it didn't seem to matter. But then I started thinking about what she might have meant."

"Right," Chloe said, clearly realising there was more to come.

Kate couldn't turn to face her, as she was driving, but she gave her voice a little added emphasis. "You're observant, Chloe. You said that yourself, and I believe you. Don't you think there's something funny about the refugee centre? Don't you think that something doesn't quite add up?"

Chloe frowned. She was silent for a moment as she thought. Then she said slowly, "Given that you've mentioned money, I'm guessing that you might be thinking—" She paused and then said slowly "If it's being generously funded by Sanctuary...then why does it look so shabby? Is that it?"

"Yes." Kate tapped her fist on the steering wheel. "Sanctuary make millions in fund raising. They've even had government grants—I looked it all up yesterday. They've got a lot of wealthy patrons and donors who don't mind shelling out a hell of a lot of cash for the cause. So, if that's the case, why is the Salterton shelter being run on a shoestring and why does it look as though it's about to collapse from lack of funding?"

Chloe was silent again, obviously running what Kate had said through her head. "It's not much though," she said eventually. "A throwaway remark..."

"I know," Kate said. "That's why we're following

up a hunch with a proper investigation. Starting with an interview."

The traffic grew heavier and heavier as they entered London and conversation necessarily ceased. Kate was unused to driving in the capital and found it more stressful than she'd imagined. Tense-jawed, she negotiated her way through unfamiliar streets, darting glances at the sat nav and trying to avoid the pedestrians who seemed likely to fling themselves in front of her car with a total lack of fear or self-preservation.

Chloe spent the time reading through the print-outs that Kate had brought with her. Once or twice, Kate heard her make a noise of surprise, but other than that, she said nothing. Kate commented that it was lucky she didn't get car sick, which elicited nothing more than a grunt from Chloe.

Eventually they reached their destination. Kate circled the block several times, looking for a suitable parking space. As she finally spotted one, and drew into the kerb, she promised herself fervently that she would never move to London.

Chloe and Kate approached the house. Chloe had put the printed papers away in her briefcase which she held in one hand. "If all this is in the public domain," she remarked as they got nearer the gates, "Then why hasn't anyone else picked up on it? Your boyfriend, for one?"

"Well, to be fair, not all of it is public knowledge," said Kate. "I had to make a few phone calls, pull a few strings. And people *have* said something, in the past. They've just been disbelieved or shouted down, from the sounds of it. I suppose, if you're charismatic enough, you can pull the wool over anyone's eyes."

"True." They had reached the front door of the house, and Chloe put her finger to the bell. Once it was answered, she snapped, "DS Wapping and DS Redman."

There was a moment of silence on the other end of the crackling line. Kate waited to see if the entry lock of the door would be buzzed but it remained silent. The two women looked at one another and Chloe raised her finger again.

"Wait." Kate caught at her arm. Her keen ear had caught the sound of footsteps approaching the door from the inside of the house.

They waited. After a moment, the door opened and Gayle Templeton stood in the doorway. She was smiling the neutral smile that all good personal assistants quickly develop, although it was possible to ascertain the faintest flicker of consternation in the pucker of her eyebrows.

Chloe snapped her warrant card in Gayle's face, close enough for the woman to recoil and blink.

"I'm afraid the Sanderbys aren't in the office at the moment," Gayle said after a moment.

"That's fine," Kate said with a smile. She felt an

inappropriate leap of glee. It wasn't often she was actually able to play good cop, bad cop. "It's actually you we'd like to talk to, Miss Templeton. May we come in?"

"Me?" Gayle looked shocked, and Chloe took advantage of her confusion by pressing forward. The other woman automatically stepped back and then both Kate and Chloe were in the hallway of the Sanctuary offices.

"I'm—I'm not sure how I can help you," said Gayle. The tiny stutter betrayed her nervousness.

"Oh, we just want a bit of a chat, that's all," Kate said breezily. Chloe stood silent, a stony look on her face. Kate saw Gayle shoot her a quick, jittery glance. "Perhaps we can go through into the office?"

The office looked much as it had the first time they had visited. The fire was lit and two tall beautiful vases of fresh flowers stood at either end of the mantelpiece. Kate looked at the display. There must have been a hundred red roses between the two bunches, each bud curled and perfect as a whorl of damp red velvet. She thought again about the sitting room at the Salterton refugee shelter, about Ruth's office, which could have doubled as a broom cupboard, and felt a renewed sense of purpose.

"So where are the Sanderbys today?" Kate asked, sitting herself down in one of the comfortable armchairs without being asked.

For a moment she thought Gayle was going to

refuse to answer. Then the woman said, reluctantly, "They're at their second home by the coast. The last week has been—well, let's just say they need a bit of time to recuperate."

"Yes, I can see that," Kate said sympathetically. "It must have been very hard. Has the publicity helped at all? Or hindered?"

Gayle gave her a suspicious look. "I'm not sure what you mean."

"I mean, all the publicity about the charity, given its connection to the tragic deaths in Salterton. Has that helped the public profile at all?"

"Yeah," said Chloe, with a hint of menace. "Donations flooding in, are they?"

Gayle looked frightened at first and then haughty. "I don't see—it's been a very distressing time for all of us. Obviously, people want to help." She paused and then said bitingly, "At least there are *some* people in the world who actually want to make a difference."

"Oh, I couldn't agree more," said Kate. She had to stamp down on the feeling of wanting to needle even further. There was always a danger one would get slightly too much fun out of being able to torture a suspect. "I joined the police force because I wanted to make a difference. To other people's lives, I mean, not just my own." She felt Chloe's little flinch beside her and realised she was going a little too close to the bone. For now. "Anyway, there's a couple of points I was hoping you might help us with."

"Yes?" said Gayle, in a chilly tone.

"Firstly, could you give me the Sanderby's holiday home address?"

Gayle did so, rather reluctantly. Kate noted it down.

"How long have you worked for the Sanderbys?" she asked.

Gayle looked at her expressionlessly. "I started working for them in...er...2005."

"So your employment with them predates the formation of the charity? Of Sanctuary, I mean?"

"Yes. Yes, I suppose so."

"Sanctuary was founded in 2010, according to your website. Is that right?"

Gayle was clearly wondering where these questions were going. "Yes. I believe that's right."

Kate glanced down at her notebook, as if reading her notes. Really though, she was building tension. At times like this, she sometimes thought she should take up amateur dramatics as a hobby. "Audits."

Gayle looked blank. "Sorry?"

"Audits," Kate repeated once more. "I presume you're familiar with the term."

Gayle sounded flustered. "Yes—yes, of course, but I don't see— "

"Well, it's like this," said Kate. "Obviously, as a registered charity, I assume Sanctuary would have been audited at some point? Hmm? Would you be able to let us have a look at the reports? Just the latest one would do."

She could almost see Gayle thinking fast. As the silence lengthened, Kate took in the whole of the woman's clothes: the diamond earrings, the expensive watch on one slender wrist, the well-cut suit and what looked like designer shoes.

"Of course," Gayle said eventually. "It's been a while since the last one, so it might take me a while to find the reports." She cleared her throat. "I wouldn't want you to wait if you've got anything else to do, I can send them over to you later, if that helps."

"Oh, we don't mind waiting, do we, DS Wapping?" Kate said easily. "We'll just sit here quietly. We won't get in your way."

"Fine," Gayle said tightly. She left the room and they heard her high heels clip-clopping down the parquet flooring of the hallway.

"Tut, tut. Didn't even offer us coffee," Kate said, shaking her head.

"What's the betting she's not going to find those reports?" said Chloe.

"Oh, that's a given," said Kate. "We could wait all day and she'll still not find them. I just wanted to see her reaction when I asked for them."

Chloe smiled. "You've got an evil streak in you. I like it."

"It's well hidden," Kate said, grinning. "But it comes out to play now and again."

Chloe snorted with laughter. Then she pushed herself upright. "So, what now?"

Kate leant back in her chair. "We wait for Miss Templeton to come back empty-handed. Then we ask her a few more questions."

As it was, Gayle returned in less than twenty minutes, and to Kate's surprise, she held a folder in her hand. She was smiling again.

"I'm so sorry, but I think the audit reports are in archive," she said. "But I do have a report on the charity here from the Westminster School of Economics that I thought you might like to read."

Kate took it. "Oh, thank you so much." With difficulty, she repressed a cynical laugh. "Would you mind if we took this?"

"Not at all." Gayle seemed to have recovered her poise. "I'll arrange for the archives to send over the audit reports. That will take a few days, though."

"Thank you." Kate handed the report to Chloe, who stowed it in her briefcase. "Now, I know you're busy but I do have a quick few questions."

Gayle's professional smile flickered for an instant. "Yes?"

"May I ask your whereabouts on the night of the second of October between the hours of eleven pm and four am?"

"My whereabouts?" Gayle said blankly.

"Yes." Kate leant forward. "On the night of the

second of October between the hours of eleven pm and four am. That's the night that Ali Araya was killed."

"You can't think I had anything to do with that!"

"I just want to know where you were, Miss Templeton," Kate said mildly. "It's standard procedure in a murder investigation."

"I—I was—" Gayle stuttered. Then she seemed to take a grip on herself. "I think I was at home. Yes, I was at home. I was at home all evening."

"Did you talk to anyone? Go on social media?"

Gayle looked embarrassed. "I—I was probably on Facebook for some of the time."

"Thank you." Kate asked for the name of her Facebook profile and wrote it down. "That's great."

Gayle looked relieved. "Well, if that's everything..."

"Not quite." Kate saw the woman tense up again. "I also need to know your whereabouts on the night Nada Qabbani was killed. The night of the seventh, between the hours of eight pm and midnight."

This time Gayle didn't bother to protest. She put a hand up to her temple and rubbed it, as if smoothing away a pain. "I was here, I think. I know I've been working very late over the past month or so."

"I see." Kate scribbled a few notes. "Right, well, that's almost everything." Gayle's professional smile appeared again. "I just want to know if you know about your employers' backgrounds. That's my last question."

The smile disappeared. "Sorry?"

"Nuria and Peregrine Sanderby. Where did Nuria come from?"

"Come from?" Gayle was frowning. "She was born in Iran. Her family came over here in the seventies because her father was being persecuted for his political beliefs."

"That's what she told you, no doubt."

Gayle looked shocked again. "What do you mean?"

"I mean," said Kate. "That that is the story that Nuria Sanderby has been telling everyone since she became a celebrity."

Gayle appeared lost for words. Kate let the silence grow and then said, in a calm voice "Well, I can see that despite your long record of service, you don't know everything about your employers. We'll see ourselves out, Miss Templeton."

She turned on her heel, Chloe doing likewise and left the room. They walked in silence down the hallway and kept their counsel until the front door was closed behind them. As they reached the roadway, Kate looked back. As she expected, Gayle's pale face was watching them go.

"Lord, I'd give good money for a phone tap right now," she said as they got into the car.

"It could be arranged," said Chloe. She buckled her seatbelt. "Especially if we're going to make an arrest."

"We're not quite there yet," Kate said. She pressed the screen of the sat nav and tapped the 'go home' icon. "I still have a couple of things I'd like cleared up."

They drove away. Chloe moved the briefcase to a more comfortable position in the footwell. "So, what was with that report Gayle gave us?"

Kate laughed. "I imagine they paid for it."

"Really?"

"I expect so. Shell out twenty thousand or so and get what looks like a genuine report to back up their claims for funding."

"Blimey." Chloe looked impressed. "I should have gone into academia."

Kate negotiated her way back through South London before they could rejoin the motorway. Perhaps because it was early afternoon, the traffic had lessened a little. The sun was still shining and she felt her spirits lift at the thought of getting back to the countryside.

"So, what made you think of it?" asked Chloe. She had reclined her chair and was propping her knees on the dashboard.

Kate smiled. "It was actually a conversation I had with Tin—my boyfriend. Just a misunderstanding, but it made me realise how things might have been misconstrued and I could then apply it to that remark made by Ali Araya to Nada. He said 'she's not what you think, you know', something like that, and Nada took him to mean Ruth because he said 'the lady who runs the shelter'."

"Right," said Chloe. "But the person he was actually talking about was Nuria. Right?"

"Right." Kate checked her rear view mirror, preparing to overtake a lorry. "So once I had that, everything else started to fall into place."

Chloe was staring ahead through the windscreen. "It doesn't work, you know," she said, after a moment. "Nuria Sanderby has an unbreakable alibi for the night of Ali Araya's death. And she pretty much does for the night of Nada's death and what's his name, Peregrine, does too."

"I know," said Kate. "That's why I need to clear a few more things up."

"So where are we going?"

"I need to talk to Ruth Granger," Kate said. She pressed down harder on the accelerator and the car surged forward.

Chapter Twenty

IT WAS LATE AFTERNOON WHEN they finally got back to the West Country. Kate had been hoping that Ruth was still at Abbeyford Station but she was disappointed. Once she'd left the motorway, she'd pulled in at the first lay-by and rung Olbeck to be told that, once again, Ruth Granger had been released without charge.

"Why?" Kate demanded.

"Because her alibi for the night of Nada's death has been verified. She was in the pub she told us about from nine o'clock to nearly midnight. That's well past the time of death, so for that she's in the clear." Olbeck sounded exhausted.

"You sound knackered," Kate pointed out.

"I am. I've been interviewing since first thing this morning. I need to get home now or Jeff will divorce me."

"Give him my love," said Kate, saying goodbye. She returned the phone to her handbag and put the car into gear.

"Ruth Granger's been released without charge," she told Chloe. "I guess we'll find her at home, then."

The car sped through the splendour of the autumn day, the sun now low in the sky, bleeding scarlet into the clouds. The trees blazed with colour. Kate felt a surge of anticipation and something that could have been either excitement or unease. She was so close now... There were just a few loose ends to be tied up...

She turned the car onto the Salterton road. She was driving into the sunset, and it was hard to see through the glare. As they reached the shore road, the waves glittered and the sun laid a blood-red strip across the ocean as it sank below the horizon.

Kate found she remembered the way to Ruth Granger's flat without having to use the sat nav. She found a parking space a short distance away and pulled on the hand brake. She looked over at Chloe, who was looking thoughtful. "Ready?"

"Ready as I'll ever be." Chloe swung her long legs around and got out of the car.

The drop in temperature was noticeable as soon as Kate got out herself. Now the sun had set, the night was chilly and she hastened to grab her jacket from the back seat. Chloe was hugging her own coat closer to herself.

"Brr..."

"I know. Come on, let's get inside the flat, at least."

They climbed the short flight of stairs that led to the flat's front door. It was a modern, purpose-built building, with three stories. Ruth and Josh lived on the second. Kate knocked on the door and waited.

After a couple of minutes, she knocked again. There was no answer. Kate looked at Chloe.

"Where could she have got to? She can't be at work now, surely?" She checked her watch to be on the safe side. "Perhaps we'd better head back to the refuge, to check."

They hurried down the stairs and back to the car. Kate was conscious again of the feeling of unease. It *was* unease, not anticipation. What was the matter? She tried to put the feeling away, tried to block it out, but it kept returning.

It was only a short drive to the refugee centre. The car park was again empty, save for one or two cars parked at the far end. Kate and Chloe tried the front door of the shelter, which was locked.

"Hang on a minute." Kate left Chloe standing there and quickly walked around the building. Something had just occurred to her, and it seemed a good idea to check... She walked around to the back of the building, where Nada had approached her, and stopped in the place where, as far as she could tell, she had stood that night, the night Nada was killed. Then she looked up at the building. Yes, just as she'd thought... She felt her mouth set in a grim line.

"What's up?" Chloe asked as she walked back around to the front entrance.

"I just had to check something," answered Kate.

She gave an impatient shake of the head as Chloe opened her mouth to ask her another question. "Don't worry about it now, it was just something I had to get straight."

"Okay." Chloe shifted her weight from one foot to the other. "So where do we go now?"

"We try and find Ruth."

Chloe waved her phone. "I've already tried calling her."

"And?"

"Going through to voicemail. I've left a message."

"Okay." Kate paused for a moment, irresolute.

As if reading her mind, Chloe asked "I guess we *do* have to do this right now? It couldn't wait until tomorrow or until she contacts us?"

"Well..." Kate paused again. Looked at logically, there was no real reason for them to interview Ruth that very moment. But... Kate felt that uneasiness start to rise again, like a black, shark-fin-filled wave. "I'd just rather know where she is," she finished, a little lamely.

Luckily, Chloe appeared to be in a receptive mood. "All right," she said cheerfully. "Why don't we try that pub she was at, the night Nada was killed?"

"The Jolly Sailor, wasn't it?"

"Yes," said Chloe. "I know where it is. Come on, it's not far."

They left Kate's car in the car park, and Chloe led Kate down the street, turning off into a long, dark alleyway. There were no streetlights along the entire path and Kate hurried through it, feeling rather spooked. She was glad to get out into the street at the end, even though that was almost as ill-lit as the alleyway.

"Could do with some lights, along there," she commented to Chloe. "Looks like a haven for muggers."

Chloe glanced back at the entrance to the alleyway. "I suppose so," she said. "It's the quickest route to the High Street, though."

They found The Jolly Sailor, a rather nice looking pub, on the sea front. Kate could see why Ruth, even alone, would have found it a pleasant place to spend an evening. It wasn't a large place and it took them less than five minutes to ascertain that Ruth wasn't there.

"I'll check the loos," suggested Chloe.

Kate nodded. "I'll check with the barman."

Both enquiries turned out to be negative. Kate and Chloe conferred by the saloon door.

"What now?"

Kate hesitated. Every logical bone in her body was urging her to give it up for the night and come back to the search tomorrow, when she wasn't so tired, when Ruth might have contacted them anyway, when perhaps the last little pieces of the puzzle would have fallen into place. She opened her mouth to say something like, 'okay, let's leave it until tomorrow', and then her gut twisted and she found herself clenching her fists.

"What's up?" Chloe's keen eye had caught her expression.

"All right," Kate said, in a low voice. She pushed open the door of the pub and beckoned for Chloe to follow her. "I'm worried. I'm worried about Ruth."

Chloe frowned. "Because she knows something?"

"I don't know. I don't know what she knows, if anything. It's just—" She paused, tapping her foot against the concrete. "I'm just worried," she finished.

"Always trust your gut." Chloe pulled her coat tighter about her. It was properly cold now, a chill sea breeze blowing inland.

"I'm glad you think that," Kate said. "My gut instinct saved my life on a few occasions."

Chloe looked at her sharply, obviously wondering whether she was having her leg pulled. She realised Kate was serious. "That sounds like a few stories worth hearing over a drink." She looked back inside the inviting pub. "Should we call it a day and have a few bevvies here?"

Kate looked back into the pub, its windows glowing with a warm yellow light. The thought of going inside, settling in one of the big leather armchairs by the open fire and enjoying a good glass of red wine was immensely tempting.

Then she sighed and shook her head. "You won't know how hard it is to say no—but no." She felt her stomach jump again, and the panicky jab in the gut infused her with urgency. "I really need to find out if Ruth's okay."

"Yes, but how? We have no idea where she is. She could be anywhere."

Kate stood with her chilly hands in her pockets, thinking back over the day. The drive to London, the interview with Gayle Templeton, the drive back again... She remembered her notebook, lying on the front seat of the car.

"I know somewhere we can try," she said slowly. "But you don't have to come if you don't want to."

Chloe looked at her for a long moment in silence. "You don't think I'm letting you have all the fun?" she said eventually, with a small grin.

Kate smiled back, even over her rising unease. "Come on, then. Let's get to work."

Chapter Twenty One

As they walked back to the car, Kate became aware that a sea fog was beginning to rise, wreathing the dark streets in chilly white vapour. Air currents twisted the mist into strange patterns beneath the street lights. Cold and eerie as it was, Kate was happy to reach the relatively sanctuary of her car.

"I think I know where we're going," Chloe said, as she got in and slammed the passenger door.

Kate handed her the notebook, open at the page with the address on it. "Was it there you were thinking?"

Chloe looked grim. "Yes."

The roads were quiet but Kate couldn't drive particularly fast, given the rapidly thickening mist that drifted in blank white ribbons across the road, illuminated by the car headlights. At times, Kate had to slow the car to a crawl, unable to see more than a few feet in front of her. As the road twisted upwards to the cliffs, she slowed even further, knowing that a sheer drop to the beach below lay on one side of her. The plethora of road signs that warned of 'Danger:

Weak Cliffs. Do not approach the edge' did nothing to calm her fears.

They reached the summit of the cliff road and it flattened out. Kate drove past the carpark for Muddiford Beach, completely empty now. They went further, passing the sugar-cube house of Alan Hardcastle. Further still, through a wooded area at the top of the cliffs, where the road began to twist again as it curved gently along the lines of the coast. After five minutes' driving, Kate saw the turn off she'd been looking for.

They were about two miles inland but the road they were following ran straight towards the sea, through thick forest. It was a small road, barely two lanes, and after a minute or so, the trees on either side began to thin. Soon, Kate could see the silhouette of a house before them, a huge, white-painted box of a house, similar to the one in South London in its structure, but obviously much newer. A wide sweep of driveway ran along the front of the building and there were three cars there: a black BMW, a vintage Porsche and, incongruously, a tiny, battered Fiat. As soon as Kate saw it, she knew she'd seen it before, in the carpark of the refuge.

"Ruth's here," she whispered to Chloe and then wondered why she was whispering.

Chloe said nothing but leant forward, scanning the scene, her face tense. Kate had assumed the noise of their arrival would have meant an outside light being snapped on, perhaps the door being opened, but the front of the house remained in darkness. She drew up beside the Fiat as quietly as she could and switched off the engine.

Chloe and Kate sat there in the darkness and silence for a minute. Then Kate roused herself. "I think we should take a look around."

"Wait." Chloe was keying a number into her mobile phone. When the number she was ringing was answered, Chloe said "This is DS Wapping, I'm currently with DS Redman from Abbeyford Station. Yes. Yes—" She looked across at Kate as she spoke. "We're currently at the home of Nuria and Peregrine Sanderby, near Salterton." She gave the address. "Yes, if you could just let DCI Atwell know. He might want to inform DCI Anderton at Abbeyford. Thanks. Thanks, Mike. Talk soon."

She pressed a button on her screen to end the call and gave Kate a quick, sheepish grin. "Just in case."

"Good call." Kate was wondering why she hadn't thought to do the same thing. "Right, come on. Let's have a look around. Quietly."

There was a pathway that led around the side of the house and they followed that, creeping through the darkness. Kate was surprised that they encountered no fences, but perhaps the house was isolated enough for its owners not to bother with such rudimentary security. She took the lead, following the walls of the house, past dark windows and what was clearly the back door, until she dodged past a wheelie bin and saw clear golden light spilling from a window ahead. She motioned to Chloe to stop.

"Wait here," Kate said in a whisper. "I'll see if I can get a closer look."

She crept forward until she was level with the windowsill. Moving as cautiously as a cat burglar, she peered into the illuminated room.

It was the kitchen; a large, open-plan kitchen stretched into a huge living space. Three sofas were arranged to make three sides of a square and a large, modern open fireplace built into the wall made up the fourth side. Kate held onto the windowsill, holding her breath. She could see Nuria and Peregrine Sanderby clearly—they were sat on the far sofa, side by side, facing the woman on the sofa opposite them. Even though she'd been expecting to see her, Kate couldn't help letting out a sigh of relief. Ruth Granger was unharmed. She strained her ears to see if she could hear what they were talking about but the double-glazed windows were too thick, and nothing could be ascertained.

Kate was about to creep back to where Chloe was waiting when movement from the living room caught her eye. Nuria Sanderby had got up and was moving purposefully towards the kitchen, straight towards the window where Kate was crouching. Quickly, she drew herself back out of Nuria's line of sight and pressed herself back against the wall.

As Nuria got nearer, Kate could faintly make out what she was saying.

"—feel better for a drink, at least. Although, Ruth, I think you're a bit overwrought. The last few days have been an awful strain on all of us."

Kate could hear the chink of glasses and the noise of a bottle being uncorked. Nuria's face could be seen in profile, frowning down at whatever drinks she was preparing. Then she suddenly looked up and stared out of the window, out into the black night. The expression on her face made Kate shudder.

The moment only lasted seconds. Then Nuria was gone.

"Christ," whispered Chloe as Kate got back to her. "Did you see her face? We have to get in there."

"I know." Kate began moving towards the back door. She heard Chloe swear softly behind her as she bumped into something.

Kate expected the back door to be locked. If it had been, she was torn between booting it down—never the easiest or quietest task—or withdrawing and waiting for backup from either Abbeyford or Salterton. She let out a giant held breath as she tried the handle and it moved underneath her palm.

"Let's go," she whispered to Chloe and was swamped with a wave of gratitude that she wasn't on her own.

Once they were in the house, it was easy to navigate by the sound of voices. The back door had led them through a large utility room, along a corridor that turned one way to the entrance hall and the other way past an enormous sitting room, and what looked like another office, before leading them into the kitchen. The Sanderbys and Ruth were engrossed in their argument, and Kate and Chloe had the element of surprise. They were by the sofas before Nuria Sanderby could give more than an exclamation of surprise.

It was Peregrine that Kate had been watching. She saw the shock on his face as they appeared but that could have been natural. What she leapt on afterwards was the briefest look of fear, so brief it was almost unnoticeable unless someone had been watching closely.

It was he who spoke first. "Detective Sergeant Redman! Detective Sergeant Wapping—what a pleasant surprise." Kate could see him fitting his usual persona over him like a well-worn suit. She was impressed by the way he even managed to make his eyes twinkle. "Can I offer you a drink? How can we help you?"

Nuria said nothing. Her momentary surprise at their appearance was gone, tucked away under a face like a blank mask. Looking at her, remembering the expression she'd seen at window in contrast to the stony neutrality she could see now, Kate realised now how certain things had actually been done.

"This is not a social call," Kate said evenly. She

had realised that the back wall of the living space was actually an enormous expanse of glass, clearly designed that way to take in all of the sea views. Now, all that could be seen in the dark expanse was the white ghostly drifting of the sea mist.

Kate glanced at Ruth. She was looking thinner than ever but her high cheekbones were stained red and her hands were clutching the edge of her jumper as if it were the only thing keeping her upright.

"Miss Granger, I wish you had come to see us first," was all that Kate said to her.

Ruth gave her a furious glance. "Why? What possible bloody help could you be? You think I killed Ali, for a start!"

"No, I don't." Kate glanced over at Chloe, who shifted position very slightly, stabilising herself.

Kate turned to Peregrine, who was smiling rather anxiously. "Peregrine Sanderby, I'm arresting you for the murder of Ali Araya. You do not have to say anything, but it may harm your defence if you do not mention, when questioned, something which you later rely on in court. Anything you do say may be given in evidence."

In the ringing silence that followed, Kate turned to Nuria Sanderby. "Nuria Sanderby. I'm arresting you for the murder of Nada Qabbani." She continued with the words of caution she'd just given to Nuria's husband. "I'd like you both to accompany me and DS Wapping to the police station."

There was another silence, broken by Nuria's snort of derision. "This is preposterous," she said. "Totally ridiculous. You're clearly deluded."

"Is that all you wish to say?" Kate asked.

Nuria had gone white with anger. "I've never heard anything so ridiculous in my life. As I have clearly stated, in my interviews with your officers, I was in London at a fundraising dinner on the night poor Nada died."

"That's true," said Kate. "You were at a fundraising dinner in London. But you got there late." She felt Chloe shift a little and looked over at her colleague. "DS Wapping said the same thing, Mrs Sanderby. How there wouldn't have been time for you to kill Nada, take her to Muddiford Beach, put her handbag at the top of the cliff, dump her body over the side and still make it up to London in time for your dinner."

"Well, then," said Nuria, tightly. "What in God's name do you mean by accusing—"

Kate went on relentlessly. "There wouldn't have been time for all that, *then*. But there was ample time for you to intercept Nada on her walk back from the refugee centre, kill her, and take her body with you up to London. Probably in the boot of your car. Then you could come back down here, after your dinner, hurl her over the cliff at Muddiford and hope everyone would write it off as a suicide."

The silence that followed was even more tortuous

than the last. Kate saw Nuria's smooth olive throat ripple as she swallowed.

"It would take a special kind of person to do that," Kate went on, watching Nuria's face. "Someone who could quite cold-bloodedly think their way out of a situation like that, in order to preserve the status quo. That takes a special sort of ego. The sort of ego that might possibly belong to a liar and a fantasist, and someone who's been successfully pulling the wool over the eyes of the public for quite some time."

Peregrine Sanderby had said nothing all the while. After Kate had cautioned him, he had gradually seemed to shrink in upon himself, like a pricked balloon. The jaunty embroidered waistcoat he was wearing suddenly seemed rather pathetic.

"So, I know you killed Nada because she knew too much about Ali Araya for her own good," said Kate, speaking to Nuria. "Or you thought she did, which was the same thing in your mind. But—" She turned to Peregrine. "I'm still somewhat in the dark about why Ali had to die. I thought it was because he found out that the founders of Sanctuary had been siphoning off huge amounts of cash donated to the charity for their own personal use. But I'm still at a bit of a loss, to be honest. Can you enlighten me?"

She waited, not altogether convinced that Peregrine would actually speak. But she'd underestimated him. He raised a haggard face to her, a man suddenly grown twenty years older.

"It was an accident," he said, painfully, as if the words were being wrenched out of him. "I didn't mean for it to happen. But he asked to meet me, that night, and—I don't know—I knew he meant business."

"By business, you mean blackmail?" Kate asked, in as casual a tone as she could make it. Ruth made a sudden movement and a noise of protest, and Kate shot her a quelling look.

Peregrine said heavily, "I don't know if I would put it exactly like that. I don't—I never—we talked. He wanted money, that was true, but I don't know how much he knew about... about the money we'd—we'd taken." He swallowed as if something large was stuck in his throat. "I wasn't going to give him what he wanted. We—we argued and he—he said—he taunted me—"

He broke down then, hiding his face in his shaking hands. His lion's mane of hair fell forward over his face. Kate waited.

After a few moments, Peregrine raised his wet face. "He—he said he was sleeping with my wife." Kate heard Ruth gasp and willed her to be quiet. "He laughed and I—I lost my temper..." He looked at Kate almost fearfully. "I never meant to kill him. I shouldn't have done it but I never meant to kill him."

Kate nodded. She remembered how she and Chloe had discussed the case, days ago now, wondering whether it had been premeditated. And this fitted. Peregrine had attacked Ali with the only weapon to hand: his torch.

218

"What about the clothes?" Kate asked, a harder note creeping into her voice. Peregrine gulped and rubbed his eyes. "Let me see if I can guess. Horrified at what you'd done, you called Nuria, and she took charge, right? She suggested getting some of the clothes from the refugee centre and dressing the body in them, leaving it on the beach so we would think he was a drowned asylum seeker, perhaps?" She glanced at Nuria's stony face. "You know, Nuria, this speaks volumes about the kind of person you are. Your lover had just been killed and your first reaction is to make him back into a refugee. That's all he was ever going to be for you, wasn't it? Not a person, not a real human being, just a refugee."

Nuria said nothing. Kate had the fanciful thought that she was addressing someone who was no longer human, someone petrified into stone, a blank-faced statue.

She had almost forgotten Ruth. The grey-haired woman had sat silently through the revelations, that single gasp her only reaction. Kate opened her mouth to repeat her demand that the Sanderbys accompany her to the police station. She didn't get to say a single word.

Without a sound, Ruth hurled herself across the room and onto Nuria, her hands clawing and slashing at the other woman's face. As the two of them fell back against the sofa, sound came abruptly back. As Nuria cried out in shock, Ruth screamed at her in a voice so

219

choked with fury that only every second or third word was intelligible.

"*You.... bitch....Ali....hate....bitch...kill you!*"

At the moment of Ruth's attack, everyone had frozen with shock. Now they all ran to separate the two women, Chloe and Kate on one side, Peregrine, his face ghastly, on the other. Ruth fought all of them with a strength that belied her thin and vulnerable frame. The frenzy of her attack had already opened a wound three inches long, on Nuria's cheek, which was bleeding profusely.

"Let her *go*," roared Kate, and with Chloe's help she yanked the screaming, spitting woman back. Ruth clutched a hank of Nuria's black hair in one clenched fist.

"Hold—her—down," Kate panted, but Chloe was already doing just that, half lying over Ruth's struggling body, one knee in the small of her back. Kate could hear her talking to Ruth in a calm but shaking voice—*take it easy, Ruth, take it easy*—but it didn't look as if Ruth was taking much notice.

Relieved that it looked as though Chloe had Ruth under control, Kate turned back to the Sanderbys. The moment Ruth had been taken away from Nuria, Peregrine had released his wife like a hot coal. He sat back against the furthest corner of the sofa, as if he couldn't get far enough away from her, and buried his face in his hands, his greyish-golden hair falling forward like a veil.

Kate's eyes met Nuria's. The other woman sat there with one hand up to her bleeding cheek, her dark eyes wide. Again, Kate opened her mouth to say something, but once more she was denied. In a split second, Nuria was up and running.

"No!" yelled Kate. Peregrine didn't react as his wife ran past him, propelling herself across the room. Kate made a futile lunge, knowing she would miss and she did. Nuria ran to the great expanse of glass at the far edge of the room. For a moment, Kate thought she would crash straight through—she heard herself give a horrified gasp of anticipation as the thought struck her—but then Nuria reached for a handle, almost invisible in the dark, and slid one of the glass panels aside. A rush of cold air came into the room as Nuria ran out into the mist and the darkness.

Instinctively, Kate gave chase. Criminals ran, police officers chased; that was burnt into you from the moment you joined the force. She ran out through the open glass door and into the eddy of mist that marked the place Nuria had just passed. The light from the living room didn't penetrate far. Within twenty yards, the darkness was almost complete. Kate ran a little further and then stopped. Where the hell was she? Where the hell was Nuria? She looked down and saw a water-bejewelled lawn where the drops were rapidly turning to frost. An edge of a flowerbed showed in the corner of her vision. So, she was still in the garden then... Kate looked back, trying to orientate herself. The house, from the distant glow in the mist, seemed to be directly behind her. Had Nuria run forward? Kate held her breath, trying to locate the other woman by sound alone. She heard the crash of waves somewhere up ahead. The edge of the cliff couldn't be too far... Kate walked forward cautiously, her hands out in front of her.

Her palms met the rough prickle of a hedge. Kate stepped forward, noting there was a gap in the hedge, and a narrow path that led forward into the mist. The mud on the path showed faint footprints. Kate crouched down to look more closely. What had Nuria been wearing on her feet? She couldn't remember. As she got up, she heard the sudden snap of a twig up ahead, and her head jerked up as she tried to see through blind darkness.

"Nuria," she called, wondering whether it was a stupid thing to do to alert the other woman to her presence. Would Nuria attack her? She'd showed herself to be pretty ruthless... Kate held her breath, swinging her gaze from one way to another, trying to see if she could see her.

Was there faint, rapid breathing up ahead? Kate walked forward like a person playing Blind Man's Buff, hands held up in front of her. She stopped after ten paces. The roar of the sea was louder still. Where the hell was the cliff edge? Where was Nuria?

Distantly, she could hear the scream of sirens. The

other officers from Salterton or Abbeyford were on their way... It was almost over...

She opened her mouth to call again and then, miraculously, the mist cleared. No more than ten feet away, Nuria stood, outlined against the black sky by the faint light cast by the house. She was standing right on the edge of the cliff, facing Kate, her face no longer a neutral mask but distorted with some sort of powerful emotion. It could have been fear or anger, it was impossible to say. Blood had sheeted down her face and neck and blotched the white linen of her shirt in a pattern of gory sunbursts.

Kate's stomach bounced. For a second, she was right back there in time, her first case in Abbeyford, the kidnap of the Fullman baby. Standing on the edge of a roof, facing down a murderer. She had to stop what had happened then happening again. No matter what this woman had done.

"Nuria," she said, wishing her voice would stop shaking. "Come with me. I can help you."

Nuria said nothing. Behind her, Kate heard footsteps and a rush of cold night air. Chloe's voice said quietly behind her, "The team are nearly here."

Kate hadn't turned. She said again to Nuria, "We can help you, Nuria. Don't do this."

Still Nuria said nothing. Kate saw her shift her weight just a little from foot to foot. In the silence that filled the frosty air, came a noise, an innocent little rattle of a stone falling through space. Without even thinking about it, Kate tensed. An animal part of her brain, a muscle memory rather than a thought, made her throw herself backwards just as the ground collapsed ahead of her. All she saw as she hurled herself back through the night was Nuria's white arms go up towards the sky and the dark veil of her hair whip upwards as she fell. Kate landed hard on her side, winded, and then Chloe was dragging her, dragging her back from the edge and Nuria's scream, as she dropped, was lost in the roar of rocks and earth tumbling towards the beach far below.

Chapter Twenty Two

THE MAIN INCIDENT ROOM AT Salterton Police Station was smaller than the one at Abbeyford. It seemed even smaller now, due to the amount of people crammed into it. Kate sat with Olbeck, Chloe to one side of her. Both teams sat with each other, mingled, facing the two Chief Inspectors, who stood at the front of the room. Looking around the room, Kate thought of all the animosity that had been there at the beginning of the case and how it had slowly dissipated as they learned to work together. She remembered the feel of Chloe's strong hands dragging her back from the crumbling edge of the cliff by the Sanderbys' house. It probably wasn't too much of an exaggeration to say that Chloe had saved her life.

Thinking this, she gave Chloe a little nudge with her elbow, and as the other woman turned, eyebrows raised, Kate gave her a wink and a smile that she hoped expressed her heartfelt gratitude. Chloe's mouth quirked up at one corner and she gave Kate a poke back with one finger, which almost made Kate laugh out loud.

"Would you two cut it out?" DCI Atwell asked, sounding irritated. "You're not at school anymore."

"Sorry," Kate said contritely. She caught Anderton's gaze and they exchanged a grin behind Atwell's back.

Atwell coughed huffily and carried on talking. "Thanks for coming, all of you. It seemed apt to finish this case off with us all here together. It was due to all of your hard work that we now have a confession."

Kate's gaze wandered to the whiteboards behind Atwell and Anderton. The beautiful, haughty face of Nuria Sanderby stared back at her. It was a publicity shot—the photographer had lit her with some kind of misty light that made her white clothes glow. Like an angel, Kate thought. How ironic.

"As you know, there's going to be a full scale fraud investigation into the running of Sanctuary," Atwell was explaining. "So we could very well see Peregrine Sanderby back in court for that, as well for murder."

"Not to mention that bitch of a secretary," Chloe murmured to Kate, who nodded.

Atwell looked over at Anderton. "Want to add anything, Anderton?"

Anderton nodded, looking serious. "One thing I would say is that you all have probably gathered that there's going to be an internal investigation. It's standard procedure when there's a death of a suspect, even in pursuit rather than custody." He looked at

Kate. "So be aware that quite a few of you will be called on to give evidence in that."

"I know." Kate didn't point out that it wasn't the first time she'd had to go through that.

"Fine. It'll be fine, anyway, I'm sure. There's nothing that points to it being anything other than a tragic accident."

The meeting broke up soon after that, and the officers drifted into little knots, talking amongst themselves. Kate found herself over by the coffee machine with Olbeck, Chloe and Theo.

"Who wants one?" Chloe asked, gesturing to the machine. They all indicated that they did and she set to work with cups and coffee pods.

"Cor," Theo said appreciatively, as he took his first sip. "This is way better than the crap we get at Abbeyford."

"You'd better put in for a transfer, then," Chloe said with a grin. Kate watched as their gaze met and held for what was a second too long for casualness. She looked down quickly, smiling inwardly.

There was a slightly awkward pause and then Olbeck said, "So, Ali Araya wasn't actually killed because he knew about the embezzlement?"

"No," said Kate. "Peregrine was telling the truth. Ali had been having an affair with Nuria for several months. She was the one who gave him that Apple watch. A lover's gift."

"So, when he gave it to Nada, he meant it was

an insurance policy because—what? They could sell it? Or that he could use it to blackmail Nuria if necessary?"

Kate shrugged. "I don't know. But I think he met Peregrine that night on the beach because he did need money. Perhaps Nuria had let something slip, about the money or the fact that she wasn't ever actually an asylum seeker. He knew *something* that he thought the Sanderbys would pay good money to be kept quiet."

"She wasn't actually an asylum seeker?" Theo repeated, eyes wide.

Kate shook her head. "Total fabrication. She took the name of someone who had actually *been* an asylum seeker, back in the eighties. Changed her name by deed poll when she was seventeen. She actually grew up in care, in the North of England."

"How do you know all this?"

Kate smiled. "I did a lot of digging. Read all the interviews, Made a lot of phone calls." She paused. "Actually, it was there for people to find, if they'd looked hard enough. I can understand it, actually. She didn't want to be who she was. So she found somebody else to be." She thought, with an inner sigh, of how she herself had once been Kelly Redman. "Tell people that's who you are and why wouldn't they believe you? Eventually you start believing it yourself."

She fell silent. She could feel Chloe looking at her keenly and wondered whether she was thinking about what Kate had once told her, about her childhood. She found herself wondering whether Chloe had been in the same situation.

"Anyway," Kate said, wanting to change her train of thought. "For what it's worth, I think their original intentions were good. The Sanderbys, I mean. I think they did genuinely want to help, at first."

"Maybe," said Chloe, in a cynical tone.

"Trouble is, money goes to your head, doesn't it?" Olbeck gestured with one hand, putting a finger to his temple. "Imagine how it must have been, suddenly one day you're in charge of a charity that has millions of pounds flowing towards it, and because you've made so many friends in high places, you don't even have to be accountable for it. The temptation to start dipping into the funds, now and again..."

"And then, all of a sudden, you're in it up to your neck," Kate finished for him.

"Yes," Olbeck said. "I have a feeling we've only uncovered the tip of the iceberg, money-wise."

"Sounds like something Tin could get his teeth into," Chloe suggested.

"Yes." Kate was silent for a moment. Tin had returned to Abbeyford on the night of all the drama but she hadn't seen him yet. He'd sent a strange, rather terse text telling her he needed to see her tonight. She had the feeling he was building up to telling her something momentous and wondered whether she was ready to hear it. She sighed inwardly and tried to put the thought from her mind.

"I'm wondering if the reason Ali needed money was to help Nada," she said out loud. "Nada was worried sick about her sister, back in Syria. It wouldn't surprise me to hear that Nada was planning to get her sister out too, if she could raise the cash."

"That's pure conjecture," protested Chloe. "You can't possibly know that."

"No, I know." Kate gave in. "Ruth might be able to tell us more."

They were all silent for a moment. There had been some discussion amongst the DCIs as to whether Ruth should be charged with perverting the cause of justice, but, to Kate's relief, they had decided not to pursue it.

"She knew something was wrong with how Sanctuary was being run," she said to Chloe, as they drifted back to Chloe's desk. "She knew that there was a discrepancy."

"That's why you wanted to talk to her, that night, didn't you?"

Kate raised one shoulder in a half shrug. "Sort of. I was just worried about her, to be honest. I thought—if she knew something that Nuria wanted to keep a secret—she was in danger."

They had reached Chloe's desk now. Kate put her empty mug down on its surface.

"Thanks for the coffee," she said, realising as she did so that the rest of the team were preparing to leave.

"That's okay." Chloe stood a little awkwardly, something obviously on her mind. Then she stuck her hand out to Kate rather abruptly. "Well. It's been—interesting."

Kate shook her hand. "It's certainly been that."

There was another awkward pause and then Chloe said gruffly, "If you ever want to go out, you know, have a drink or something..."

"I'd like that." Kate hesitated and then, giving in to the impulse, pulled the other woman into a hug. For a moment, Chloe stiffened and then, tentatively, her hands came around to Kate's back and patted her shoulders.

They released each other. "See you," said Kate.

"Yeah. See you."

Kate smiled and walked away. Olbeck was waiting for her at the door.

"She's all right, you know," he said, in a tone of surprise.

Kate looked back at Chloe, who gave her a slightly embarrassed wave. "*I* know that. Come on, let's get back."

*

THE NIGHT WAS VERY COLD, winter setting in in earnest. Kate hurried towards the welcoming warm glow of The Black Cat, the bar on the High Street where she and Tin had first met. As she pulled the door open, she felt a sudden qualm that perhaps he was going to ask her to marry him. Don't be ridiculous, she scolded herself, but the thought remained, tucked away down deep.

Tin was waiting for her at their preferred table, at the back, not too far from the wood-burning stove. He was looking particularly handsome, having had his hair cut in London, and was wearing a new leather jacket with many zips and buttons.

"You look nice," Kate said, leaning over the table to kiss him.

"Thanks. So do you."

They exchanged smiles. Kate sat down and reached for the drink that Tin had already thoughtfully ordered for her.

"So—" she said, rather too brightly.

"Well done on the case," Tin said. "Must be satisfying."

"Well—" Kate paused, thinking of the three deaths, the grief, the suffering. Satisfying wasn't exactly the word she would have used. "It's—we got a solve. That's the main thing."

"Yes." Tin's right leg was jiggling. "Look," he said abruptly, and Kate felt a jab of panic. She glanced at his hands, wondering if he would suddenly reach for a small black jewellery box. What would she say if he did?

"Look," continued Tin. "You know when I was

up in London, I got through to second interview at *The Independent*?"

"Yes," said Kate.

Tin suddenly smiled. "Well, I got the job."

"Oh, that's great," Kate said sincerely and with pleasure. Just for a second, before the implications struck her. "Well done. But does that—does that mean you're moving to London?"

Tin's smile faded a little. "Actually, a bit further afield."

Kate was conscious of a slow dropping sensation. "Oh?"

Tin cleared his throat. "New York, actually. I'll be one of their State-side correspondents."

"New York," Kate said, blankly.

"Yes." Tin looked at her and then leant forward. "So—so I was wondering. Would—would you come with me?"

The shock of him asking her to marry him would have been nothing compared to this. Kate thought that, even through the roaring noise in her ears. "New York?" she said, faintly.

"I know it's a big decision," Tin said eagerly. "But what an opportunity, Kate, for both of us. Imagine living in New York? It wouldn't be forever, just a few years, but just think—oh, it would be amazing, wouldn't it? What do you think?"

"I—I—" At that moment, Kate couldn't think. Images flashed before her eyes: her little house,

Olbeck, Merlin, Jay and Laura, the green hills surrounding Abbeyford. Anderton.

"I'm not asking for an answer right now." Tin put his hand forward and took hers. "But I'm just asking you not to dismiss it right out of hand. Would you just think about it? Please?"

Kate looked up, into his handsome face. Saw the excitement and, yes, the love in his eyes. She had so many questions that she couldn't even begin to start articulating them. What would she do for a job? Where would they live? Would she even be able to get a visa? What—how—when... For a second, she felt like jumping up and running out of the bar, just to escape the buzzing in her ears.

The feeling she'd had the previous night, facing Nuria Sanderby on the edge of a crumbling cliff, reoccurred. Here was another precipice, but what would the end result be? Would she jump or would she fling herself back from the edge? And how was she to know what would be the best outcome? Was it time to, finally, jump?

She swallowed and squeezed Tin's hand.

"I'll think about it," she said.

THE END

ENJOYED THIS BOOK? AN HONEST review left at Amazon, Goodreads, Shelfari and LibraryThing is always welcome and *really* important for indie authors. The more reviews an independently published book has, the easier it is to market it and find new readers.

You can leave a review at Amazon US here or Amazon UK here.

Want some more of Celina Grace's work for free? Subscribers to her mailing list get a free digital copy of **Requiem (A Kate Redman Mystery: Book 2)**, a free digital copy of **A Prescription for Death (The Asharton Manor Mysteries Book 2)** *and* a free PDF copy of her short story collection **A Blessing From The Obeah Man.**

Requiem (A Kate Redman Mystery: Book 2)

WHEN THE BODY OF TROUBLED teenager Elodie Duncan is pulled from the river in Abbeyford, the case is at first assumed to be a straightforward suicide. Detective Sergeant Kate Redman is shocked to discover that she'd met the victim the night before her death, introduced by Kate's younger brother Jay. As the case develops, it becomes clear that Elodie was murdered. A talented young musician, Elodie had been keeping some strange company and was hiding her own dark secrets.

As the list of suspects begin to grow, so do the questions. What is the significance of the painting Elodie modelled for? Who is the man who was seen with her on the night of her death? Is there any connection with another student's death at the exclusive musical college that Elodie attended?

As Kate and her partner Detective Sergeant Mark Olbeck attempt to unravel the mystery, the dark undercurrents of the case threaten those whom Kate holds most dear...

A Prescription for Death (The Asharton Manor Mysteries: Book 2) – a novella

"I had a surge of kinship the first time
I saw the manor, perhaps because
we'd both seen better days."

IT IS 1947. ASHARTON MANOR, once one of the most beautiful stately homes in the West Country, is now a convalescent home for former soldiers. Escaping the devastation of post-war London is Vivian Holt, who moves to the nearby village and begins to volunteer as a nurse's aide at the manor. Mourning the death of her soldier husband, Vivian finds solace in her new friendship with one of the older patients, Norman Winter, someone who has served his country in both world wars. Slowly, Vivian's heart begins to heal, only to be torn apart when she arrives for work one day to be told that Norman is dead.

It seems a straightforward death, but is it? Why did a particular photograph disappear from Norman's possessions after his death? Who is the sinister figure who keeps following Vivian? Suspicion and doubts begin to grow and when another death occurs, Vivian begins to realise that the war may be over but the real battle is just beginning...

A Blessing From The Obeah Man

DARE YOU READ ON? HORRIFYING, scary, sad and thought-provoking, this short story collection will take you on a macabre journey. In the titular story, a honeymooning couple take a wrong turn on their trip around Barbados. The Mourning After brings you a shiversome story from a suicidal teenager. In Freedom Fighter, an unhappy middle-aged man chooses the wrong day to make a bid for freedom, whereas Little Drops of Happiness and Wave Goodbye are tales of darkness from sunny Down Under. Strapping Lass and The Club are for those who prefer, shall we say, a little meat to the story...

JUST GO TO CELINA'S WEBSITE to sign up. It's quick, easy and free. Be the first to be informed of promotions, giveaways, new releases and subscriber-only benefits by subscribing to her (occasional) newsletter. www.celinagrace.com.

Twitter: @celina__grace
Facebook: www.facebook.com/authorcelinagrace

More books by Celina Grace...

Hushabye (A Kate Redman Mystery: Book 1)

ON THE FIRST DAY OF her new job in the West Country, Detective Sergeant Kate Redman finds herself investigating the kidnapping of Charlie Fullman, the newborn son of a wealthy entrepreneur and his trophy wife. It seems a straightforward case... but as Kate and her fellow officer Mark Olbeck delve deeper, they uncover murky secrets and multiple motives for the crime.

Kate finds the case bringing up painful memories of her own past secrets. As she confronts the truth about herself, her increasing emotional instability threatens both her hard-won career success and the possibility that they will ever find Charlie Fullman alive...

Hushabye is the book that introduces
Detective Sergeant Kate Redman. Available
as a FREE download from Amazon Kindle.

Imago (A Kate Redman Mystery: Book 3)

"THEY DON'T FEAR ME, QUITE the opposite. It makes it twice as fun... I know the next time will be soon, I've learnt to recognise the signs. I think I even know who it will be. She's oblivious of course, just as she should be. All the time, I watch and wait and she has no idea, none at all. And why would she? I'm disguised as myself, the very best disguise there is."

A known prostitute is found stabbed to death in a shabby corner of Abbeyford. Detective Sergeant Kate Redman and her partner Detective Sergeant Olbeck take on the case, expecting to have it wrapped up in a matter of days. Kate finds herself distracted by her growing attraction to her boss, Detective Chief Inspector Anderton – until another woman's body is found, with the same knife wounds. And then another one after that, in a matter of days.

Forced to confront the horrifying realisation that a serial killer may be preying on the vulnerable women of Abbeyford, Kate, Olbeck and the team find themselves in a race against time to unmask a terrifying murderer, who just might be hiding in plain sight...

Buy Imago on Amazon, available now.

Snarl (A Kate Redman Mystery: Book 4)

A RESEARCH LABORATORY OPENS ON the outskirts of Abbeyford, bringing with it new people, jobs, prosperity and publicity to the area – as well as a mob of protesters and animal rights activists. The team at Abbeyford police station take this new level of civil disorder in their stride – until a fatal car bombing of one of the laboratory's head scientists means more drastic measures must be taken...

Detective Sergeant Kate Redman is struggling to come to terms with being back at work after long period of absence on sick leave; not to mention the fact that her erstwhile partner Olbeck has now been promoted above her. The stakes get even higher as a multiple murder scene is uncovered and a violent activist is implicated in the crime. Kate and the team must put their lives on the line to expose the murderer and untangle the snarl of accusations, suspicions and motives.

Available now from Amazon.

Chimera (A Kate Redman Mystery: Book 5)

THE WEST COUNTRY TOWN OF Abbeyford is celebrating its annual pagan festival, when the festivities are interrupted by the discovery of a very decomposed body. Soon, several other bodies are discovered but is it a question of foul play or are these deaths from natural causes?

It's a puzzle that Detective Sergeant Kate Redman and the team could do without, caught up as they are in investigating an unusual series of robberies. Newly single again, Kate also has to cope with her upcoming Inspector exams and a startling announcement from her friend and colleague DI Mark Olbeck...

When a robbery goes horribly wrong, Kate begins to realise that the two cases might be linked. She must use all her experience and intelligence to solve a serious of truly baffling crimes which bring her up against an old adversary from her past...

Buy Chimera (A Kate Redman Mystery: Book 5) from Amazon, available now.

Echo (A Kate Redman Mystery: Book 6)

THE WEST COUNTRY TOWN OF Abbeyford is suffering its worst floods in living memory when a landslide reveals the skeletal remains of a young woman. Detective Sergeant Kate Redman is assigned to the case but finds herself up against a baffling lack of evidence, missing files and the suspicion that someone on high is blocking her investigation...

Matters are complicated by her estranged mother making contact after years of silence. As age-old secrets are uncovered and powerful people are implicated, Kate and the team are determined to see justice done. But at what price?

Now available from Amazon.

Creed (A Kate Redman Mystery: Book 7)

JOSHUA WIDCOMBE AND KAYA TRENT were the golden couple of Abbeyford's School of Art and Drama; good-looking, popular and from loving, stable families. So why did they kill themselves on the grassy stage of the college's outdoor theatre?

Detective Chief Inspector Anderton thinks there might be something more to the case than a straightforward teenage suicide pact. Detective Sergeant Kate Redman agrees with him, but nothing is certain until another teenager at the college kills herself, quickly followed by yet another death. Why are the privileged teens of this exclusive college killing themselves? Is this a suicide cluster?

As Kate and the team delve deeper into the case, secrets and lies rear their ugly heads and Abbeyford CID are about to find out that sometimes, the most vulnerable people can be the most deadly...

Available now from Amazon.

CELINA GRACE'S PSYCHOLOGICAL THRILLER, **LOST Girls** is also available from Amazon:

Twenty-three years ago, Maudie Sampson's childhood friend Jessica disappeared on a family holiday in Cornwall. She was never seen again.

In the present day, Maudie is struggling to come to terms with the death of her wealthy father, her increasingly fragile mental health and a marriage that's under strain. Slowly, she becomes aware that there is someone following her: a blonde woman in a long black coat with an intense gaze. As the woman begins to infiltrate her life, Maudie realises no one else appears to be able to see her.

Is Maudie losing her mind? Is the woman a figment of her imagination or does she actually exist? Have the sins of the past caught up with Maudie's present... or is there something even more sinister going on?

Lost Girls is a novel from the author of **The House on Fever Street**: a dark and convoluted tale which proves that nothing can be taken for granted and no-one is as they seem.

Currently available on Amazon.

THE HOUSE ON FEVER STREET is the first psychological thriller by **Celina Grace**.

Thrown together in the aftermath of the London bombings of 2005, Jake and Bella embark on a passionate and intense romance. Soon Bella is living with Jake in his house on Fever Street, along with his sardonic brother Carl and Carl's girlfriend, the beautiful but chilly Veronica.

As Bella tries to come to terms with her traumatic experience, her relationship with Jake also becomes a source of unease. Why do the housemates never go into the garden? Why does Jake have such bad dreams and such explosive outbursts of temper?

Bella is determined to understand the man she loves but as she uncovers long-buried secrets, is she putting herself back into mortal danger?

The House on Fever Street is the first psychological thriller from writer Celina Grace – a chilling study of the violent impulses that lurk beneath the surfaces of everyday life.

Shortlisted for the 2006 Crime Writers' Association Debut Dagger Award.

Currently available on Amazon.

EXTRA SPECIAL THANKS ARE DUE TO MY WONDERFUL ADVANCE READERS TEAM...

THESE ARE MY 'SUPER READERS' who are kind enough to beta read my books, point out my more ridiculous mistakes, spot any typos that have slipped past my editor and best of all, write honest reviews in exchange for advance copies of my work. Many, many thanks to you all.

If you fancy being an Advance Reader, just drop me a line at celina@celinagrace.com and I'll add you to the list. It's completely free, and you can unsubscribe at any time.

Further Information

Useful sites and information for anyone who would like to assist in humanitarian aid for refugees:

Doctors of the World
The Jungle Library
Calais Migrant Solidarity

ACKNOWLEDGEMENTS

MANY THANKS TO ALL THE following splendid souls:

Chris Howard for the brilliant cover designs; Andrea Harding for editing and proofreading; Tammi Lebrecque for virtual assistanace; lifelong Schlockers and friends David Hall, Ben Robinson and Alberto Lopez; Ross McConnell for advice on police procedural and for also being a great brother; Kathleen and Pat McConnell, Anthony Alcock, Naomi White, Mo Argyle, Lee Benjamin, Bonnie Wede, Sherry and Amali Stoute, Cheryl Lucas, Georgia Lucas-Going, Steven Lucas, Loletha Stoute and Harry Lucas, Helen Parfect, Helen Watson, Emily Way, Sandy Hall, Kristýna Vosecká, Katie D'Arcy, Vanessa and of course my wonderful and ever-loving Chris, Mabel, Jethro and Isaiah.

Especial thanks to Jacky Martin, for allowing me to use her true story about rescuing refugee children from the sea in Greece.